Beneath the

Marble

BENEATH THE MARBLE

Erik Midgarden

Chapter One

Victor Nash jammed his sun-tanned hands into the pockets of his dusty jeans and surveyed his growing crops with satisfaction. He had just finished the daily tour of his fifteen-hundred-acre farm and felt proud that the wheat he planted in April and the corn he sowed in May were doing well—very well, in fact. He was right on track for the "knee-high by the Fourth of July" farming standard. Nash Farm, his pride and joy, had been in his family for one hundred and fifty years. Life couldn't get much better. His beautiful daughter was graduating from high school later in the day. He knew he would have to leave the fields for the house soon to get ready, but Victor relished being outside with his crops. Ever since he was a boy growing up on this same farm, he helped his father take care of the wheat, corn, and soybeans year after year. He felt perfectly at home in the outdoors among the swaying plants that would eventually be ready for harvest. Victor privately wished that his daughter had the same love for farm life that he did, but her dreams were taking her to the University of Minnesota in the fall. Despite her straying from the family trade, he couldn't be prouder of her.

"Victor!"

Victor could hear his wife, Lily, calling him just fine, but he didn't turn toward her immediately. He knew perfectly well that she had come out to summon him indoors so he could clean up before Emma's graduation. He needed to shower and shave, or, according to his well-meaning woman, he wouldn't be fit to be seen at such a prestigious event, his daughter's graduation from a small North Dakota high school. Lily meant well. Victor knew that. He also knew he wouldn't be the only farmer present at the event. He certainly wouldn't be the worst-dressed if he went just as he was now. Still, though, pleasing his wife was worth the time it would take to tidy up a little.

"Victor!"

Victor did turn around this time and waved at the love of his life striding toward him through the low corn rows. She wore her own pair of dusty, figure-flattering jeans and a thin, pink button-up shirt protecting her fair skin from the summer sun. Lily's wavy, raven-black hair was pulled back in a loose ponytail that bounced behind her as she made her way towards him. Her expression bore a gentle frown. Dakota, the Nash family's German Shepard, trotted at her heels.

"I know you heard me the first time, Mister!" Lily exclaimed as she arrived in front of him and pushed playfully on his chest. "Are you too busy tending to your precious crops to pay attention to your wife?"

"These crops are our livelihood, Lily," Victor reminded her, taking both of her hands in his and holding them to his heart. "I can love both of you at the same time."

"Well, that sure is a relief." Lily smiled, then stood on her tiptoes to plant a kiss on his cheek. "You know why I'm here. I think it's about time we both got cleaned up and ready to go to Emma's graduation. We don't want to be late; we'll have to sit near the back of the auditorium if the other families get there first. Is Harry coming?"

Harrison was Victor's younger brother. He hadn't heard anything about Harry wanting to come to Emma's graduation, but he wasn't one to let people know about his plans beforehand. Unpredictable and fun-loving, he lived moment-to-moment.

"We'll have to wait and see," Victor said.

Lily laughed.

"Okay, if you say so. You know, we *could* give him a call…"

"Or… we could *not.*"

Lily let her hands slip out of his and led Victor and the dog in the direction of the farmhouse—a white rectangle in the distance. In the spring, Victor could see most of the farm yard from any point in his fields since the plants were just beginning to grow. The storage shed held his hand-operated tools. Close to the farmhouse stood a traditionally painted red barn where Victor kept all of his big machinery when it wasn't in use. Victor didn't need hired help beyond what Lily and, occasionally, his brother Harry provided. He hired seasonally for pest and weed control, but with that exception, he was the sole owner and operator.

"Take off your boots before coming in the house," Lily instructed as the three ascended the three steps to the rickety, weatherbeaten front porch of their home. "Dakota stays outside. I just swept."

"You got it."

Victor obediently untied his work boots and left them next to the doormat as his wife let herself inside. As an added measure against her scolding him, he slapped his jeans clean. He didn't want to be told that he wasn't allowed near the furniture in his own house.

The screen door creaked open and slapped shut as he entered. The white front door behind stood open to let a breeze through the screen and into the house. God's air conditioning. Victor planned to budget for central air for the house. Harry frequently complained that Victor and Lily were behind the times when he came over to help his brother with extra Nash Farm work. Victor thought opening up the windows and doors in the little farmhouse was just about enough. Almost, anyway.

Although furnished with a few family heirlooms, the cozy interior held chairs and tables constructed by Victor's father, who somehow found time for woodworking in addition to farming. Lily kept wildflowers in vases in nearly every room. She cleaned as well as anyone could who lived in a rural farm house. The worn floorboards of the front entry felt smooth beneath Victor's stocking feet. He thought, *How does she manage when I spend most of my time spreading dust and grime everywhere I go? She breaks her back to pick up the mess I leave.*

"Do you want to shower first, or should I?" Lily called from the kitchen. Instead of shouting a reply, Victor walked into the kitchen. She was throwing together a turkey sandwich, which Victor knew, without asking, was for him. There was no guarantee of food at the graduation ceremony, and Lily knew that Victor got a little irritable when he was hungry. Lily noticed he had eaten little that day, and he blessed her for being so observant.

"You can shower," Victor said, sitting down at the round kitchen table. There were four matching chairs and one from a yard sale that no one ever used. There were never enough guests to fill all of them. "I'll sit here and enjoy the sandwich you're making."

"Oh, you think this is for you?" Lily asked, raising an eyebrow at him and taking a big bite out of the sandwich. She almost had Victor fooled, but then she set the rest of the sandwich on a plate and crossed the room to drop it in front of him. "Eat fast, babe. We don't want Emma to think we're not coming."

"She's with her friends," Victor said through a mouth full of bread, cheese, and turkey. "She won't even notice if we show up. Graduations are more for parents than they are for the kids."

"Well, *I* would have noticed if my parents weren't at my graduation," Lily said, rinsing her hands off and shaking them dry over the sink. "I'm going to be quick in the shower, so you had better hustle with your lunch. I want us to be on time."

"We will, Lily. Don't worry."

Lily clearly *was* still worried, but she marched out of the room, and just minutes later, Victor heard water rushing through the pipes. A side of him that was younger than his forty-five years wanted to set his sandwich down and join her in the shower as a surprise, but he figured that neither of them would really be able to enjoy themselves if they had a deadline. So, he finished eating instead, washed his dishes, and took a shower when it was his turn. He towel-dried his dirty-blonde hair and shaved as close to his cheeks as he could manage, failing as he always did to get rid of his five o'clock shadow. It was one of the hazards of having a dark beard, even on tanned skin, he supposed.

Just as Victor had pulled on a fresh pair of jeans and donned a button-down shirt that he knew Lily liked, she poked her head into their bedroom. She was already wearing light makeup and had shoes on, a sign that she was ready and raring to leave.

"I'm coming," he told her before she had a chance to say anything. "Let me just slip on my good shoes, and I'll be on the way.

You can start the truck if you want."

Lily simply nodded and whisked away. Victor could hear her low heels clacking on the wooden floor as she left. He grabbed his own shoes, tied them, and hustled out the front door, not bothering to lock the house behind him. No occupied farmsteads were within miles of Nash Farm. The town, Hope River, counted few people as residents. Crimes committed in the Hope River area tended to be acts by people passing through. Dakota acted as their guard dog. Victor's possessions consisted of worn farm machinery, run-down buildings, and a few personal items. His wife and daughter mattered more to him than any material possessions. He left his unlocked home with optimism.

Victor paused on the front porch to give Dakota a pat and told him to guard the house before hurrying over to the idling truck. Lily waited patiently in the cab on the passenger's side when Victor joined her.

As he approached the truck, he could hear Lily leaving a voicemail to Emma, saying how proud she is of her and that they were on their way. She put down the phone as he opened the driver's side door. "I guess she didn't pick up?"

"No, but I'm sure she's just busy with her friends," she smiled at him warmly. "Are you ready?" she asked, though she must have already known the answer to her own question.

"You bet."

Victor put the truck in reverse, backed it up, and then drove down the long dirt road that eventually met up with the main road that would take him into town. Passing by his farmland on the right, Victor took in the sight of the rich black soil stretching through the fields, buried beneath the ground were the seeds of the spring wheat that Victor toiled over diligently during the past couple of weeks. As the truck bumped along, Victor noticed that he had a little knot in his chest. After considering it for a moment, he realized that it had to do with his daughter.

"I can't believe Emma's all grown up," he said, easing the truck around a dip in the road. "I knew that she would be one day, but it really snuck up on me."

"Victor, she's been growing up for her entire life! How could this just sneak up on you?" Lily's voice was incredulous, but she smiled. Victor knew that she understood.

"I guess I just look at her and I see my little girl," Victor said, shrugging as they pulled onto the main road. "She'll always be Baby Emma to me."

"Me, too," Lily said warmly. "She's our all-American girl. I'm so proud of her. I wish I had been smart enough at her age to go to college."

"Babe, you're plenty smart. Emma doesn't know what she wants to study yet; she just knows that she wants to go. I'm sure you were the same way at her age."

"No, not quite. I wanted to work. I wanted a family. I didn't even think about furthering my education like a lot of people in Hope River don't. I hope that she loves where she ends up."

"She's got a bright future," Victor predicted. "I can feel it."

Victor smiled to himself as they drove down the road. In the distance, he could see another truck rumbling towards them.

"We're going to have an empty nest," Lily sighed.

"Yeah, but at least we'll have each other," Victor reminded her. "That'll be enough for me as long as Emma remembers to call."

"Will it really?"

This caught Victor off-guard.

"What do you mean?"

"I mean, will just having me be enough for you with Emma gone? What if we don't have anything to talk about anymore? What if…?"

"Lily, love of my life, I could live anywhere and do anything as long as we stay together. I don't need anything else. I love our daughter, too, but she isn't the only reason I've stuck around all these years. We're going to be just fine."

Lily smiled, her green eyes tearing up ever so slightly.

"Do you really mean that, Victor?"

"I do. I love you. I always will."

"I love you, too, Victor. Until the day I die and beyond, nothing in the world will change that."

"Listen to us. We sound like teenagers. Speaking of teenagers," Lily pulled her ringing phone from her purse.

• • •

THE AIR AT HOPE RIVER HIGH SCHOOL'S football field hung heavy with the scent of freshly mowed turf. A large stage had been erected facing the concrete bleachers, and chairs lined the manicured field for the few dozen-some students about to graduate from high school and start their college dreams. Among a small sea of caps and gowns, Emma congregated with the rest of the students awaiting the graduation ceremony, her blonde hair nearly shining in the afternoon sun beneath her cap. She wore a special sash as this year's valedictorian, a testament to her hardworking nature and deep intelligence. Bursting with an infectious enthusiasm, she had spent her entire life in Hope River, drawing people to her effortlessly like moths to a flame. She flitted from group to group, her laughter echoing through the air as she shared her excitement with her friends.

While talking with an acquaintance, she mentioned her plans to study at the University of Minnesota in Minneapolis. "I'm actually really excited about the Community Engagement Scholars Program," Emma cooed, her jade-green eyes twinkling. "It's going to be a lot of work, 400 hours of community service, but I think it will be incredibly rewarding to make a difference outside of Hope River."

She briefly felt the vibration of her cell phone in her pocket but was whisked away by Andrea, her best friend throughout childhood, as they started taking photographs together with their many friends. After a few too many "silly ones," the students were instructed to line up and be ready to start walking to their seats once the ceremony began.

As she took her place in the line of robed teenagers, she checked her phone to see a missed call from her mother, Lily, and listened to her message saying they were on the way. A smile brightened her face at the kindness and love shown by her mother, a deep joy that forced her to calm herself before she messed up her makeup due to the tears welling up in her eyes. Scanning the relatively small crowd in the concrete bleachers, she couldn't spot her parents and decided to give her mother a dial back.

• • •

BOOM!

Very suddenly, the steering quit. The truck seemed to have a mind of its own. Lily screamed. Victor shouted back at her, something to let her know that everything was going to be okay, even though he had no idea whether or not that would be true. His foot remembered to slam on the brakes. In the instant before the brakes locked, Victor's truck swerved into the opposite lane, smashing head-on into the oncoming vehicle. There was an ear-splitting *CRUNCH!* And then, for a time, perhaps seconds or minutes or hours, there was nothing.

Victor's awareness gradually returned to the scene of the crash. When he weakly lifted his head, he blinked blearily around the remains of his truck, trying to make sense of what had happened. He turned to Lily. He hoped to see her well and wondered if she knew what happened.

"Lily? Lily!" His heart dropped.

He saw her dark hair, shiny with scarlet blood. Her body slumped against the deployed airbag. He remembered his arms and reached out, trying to shake her into consciousness, but his muscles failed to perform. His arms dropped weakly to the side. He heard sirens wailing in the distance, and he realized that they must be for Lily and for him.

This is a car wreck, he realized. *We collided with someone. But how? What happened? I don't understand.*

CHAPTER TWO

"Nice job tonight, Emma. You were on fire!"

"Thanks," Emma Nash said a little sheepishly. It felt strange to be complimented on her stripping skills, even if it was by one of her friends and fellow strippers. Clearly, she hadn't been in the game long enough to feel comfortable thinking of herself as good at taking her clothes off for pay. Since she had abandoned higher education only five months previously, Emma thought that she deserved something of a grace period when it came to adjusting to her new career choice.

"Are you on tomorrow night?" April asked, unabashedly changing out of her costume and into her street clothes. She winked and said with a smile, "It's Saturday, so lots of lonely guys ready to lose their money will be coming in."

"No, I'm actually going home to see my dad," Emma admitted, not meeting April's eyes as she tied her shoes and stuffed her lacy costume and high heels into her bag.

"You sound almost guilty about that," April mused, tucking a long, dyed-blonde curl behind her ear. "What, you don't get along with your daddy?"

"Not anymore," Emma sighed, not in the mood to play around. The truth was that a year ago, she would have loved to go home and visit her father, but he hadn't been the same since the accident. Something within him had shriveled and died with Emma's mother. While Emma wasn't exactly thriving, she had expected her dad to remain strong through the tragedy that had befallen their family. Instead, he became bitter and chose to isolate himself rather than reach out to his surviving family members for support. He cut Emma off as well, just when she needed him more than any time in her life. She refused to blame her dropping out of university on his personality shift because that wouldn't be fair. She changed herself, but losing both of her parents, either literally or metaphorically, pushed her over the edge—an edge she hadn't realized was so close.

"Hey, I didn't mean to pry or anything," April said, crossing the small changing room to put a comforting hand on Emma's shoulder. "I was just playing around. I know how family can be. I'm trying to raise two kids all by myself. Believe me, their daddy wasn't any good, either. Sometimes, women just get the raw end of the deal. It's up to us to pick ourselves up off the ground and do what we can to move forward. It's not fair, but it's the truth."

"I know," Emma forced a smile. "Thank you."

"No thanks necessary." April turned and walked as though to exit through the club's back door, but she stopped and looked at Emma once again. "Hey, Emma?"

"Yeah?"

"The track marks are starting to show up on your arms. You might want to watch out. Nobody's going to want a lap dance from a junkie."

Emma experienced the very uncomfortable combination of heat rushing up into her cheeks as her stomach dropped. She instinctively crossed her arms to hide the evidence and remembered the sweatshirt stuffed inside her locker. Her locker stood open, and she hurriedly withdrew the baby blue bundle. A warm summer night awaited her outside, but she donned the sweater anyway. April watched her without emotion. Emma wanted to tell her to quit judging. But Emma knew she shouldn't have started using heroin. She currently led a life that she would have thought unimaginable a year before. But April wasn't completely innocent herself. In fact, she was a cliché. A thousand Aprils toiled in strip clubs in Minnesota alone, and yet she dared criticize Emma for her life choices?

You're a cliché, too, you know, a part of Emma's consciousness whispered quietly into her ear. *You're a druggie college dropout who strips to support her habit. You have no right to judge anyone, either.*

"Good night, Emma."

Emma abandoned her thoughts, saw April wave, and let herself out the door. April didn't give Emma a chance to reply, which irked her, but she took a deep breath and let it go. She felt a little on edge because the cocaine that kept her going through her shift was tapering off. She sadly realized a low would follow the high she rode for most of her shift. Emma usually used coke to get through her shifts and stay skinny for work. Formerly, heroin was a special treat for a night's work. It scared her to realize she required a little of each to get her through the work night. The life she wanted? No, she wanted nothing of her present life but couldn't imagine how to change without her mother's encouragement and her father's support.

Emma slung her bag over her shoulder and walked to the little apartment she shared with Maddie, another stripper from the Phoenix Den. Maddie often worked the late night to the early morning shift. She was preparing to leave for work when Emma walked through the door. That meant it was approaching one o'clock in the morning, which was bad news for Emma's travel plans. She planned to catch the westbound train to North Dakota in the morning. She counted on her father to pick her up at the station. She hoped he would be there. He quit answering the phone and rarely responded to letters. A month before, he surprised her with an answer to a letter about her travel plans. That letter marked the first time she had heard from him in six months. She hoped that everything was going to work out for a change. Emma needed a break from her usual bad luck.

"When are you coming back, Emma?" Maddie called from the bathroom they shared. It sounded like her mouth was hanging open while she tried to speak, so Emma guessed that she must be trying to talk and apply mascara at the same time.

"I won't be gone long," Emma promised. She shuffled into the bedroom and pulled a half-full suitcase out from underneath the bed. She needed to finish packing tonight so she could sleep a little later in the morning.

"What's your dad like? Do you think he has room for another daughter in his heart?" Maddie joked.

"You can have him if you want him," Emma said, rolling her eyes and stuffing a pair of jeans she used to like to wear around the farm into her suitcase. "He's been checked out ever since my mom died."

"Oh, right. I'm sorry. Me and my big mouth."

"It's fine," Emma assured her, even though, in a way, it wasn't.

Emma had not visited the farm where she grew up since she left for college. She dropped out without consulting her father or Uncle Harry. She searched futilely for a job to support herself. Finally, she descended to stripping. She made more in a night of stripping than in a week at a minimum-wage job. She didn't permit false pride to stand in the way of a good financial deal. However, good deal or not, she refused to tell her dad. As far as he was concerned, and as far as her infrequent letters described, she was still very much enjoying life at the University of Minnesota, and it would stay that way. Now was not the time to suddenly start opening up to a parent who frankly didn't seem to care very much for her anymore.

Emma spent the next half hour packing everything that she needed for the next week and began preparing for bed. Emma had an urge to take a small bump of coke, or do something even more nefarious, but resisted, knowing she'd need to get up early in the morning to catch the train. Maddie left at some point during Emma's time packing, so Emma claimed the shower and cleaned up a bit before heading to bed. She used to shower in the morning, but ever since she started stripping, she showered immediately after work. Doing anything else after being in that club made her feel dirty.

Toweling her hair and body dry, Emma slipped into her pajamas and collapsed into bed. Her dirty towel remained in a pile on the well-trodden carpet of her room. She let her thoughts drift, doing her best to keep them from floating into dark places. Just before falling asleep, she thought she smelled her mother's perfume. For a bizarre, exhilarating moment, Emma sat bolt-upright in her bed, searching her room for the woman who had raised her. Then, she became aware once more that she was alone. She curled into a ball and lay on her side, trying to keep in the tears building behind her eyes. During lonely nights, it felt as though her mom had died only the week before. She knew being sober didn't help, but allowed herself to feel these terrible feelings. As she fell asleep once again, she wondered if it would always feel that way.

CHAPTER THREE

Victor felt the smooth, sturdy wheel of the truck beneath his calloused hands and his foot on the gas pedal as he watched a black truck approaching in the distance, the truck etched in his memory as clearly as a photograph. Out of the corner of his eye, he saw Lily's mouth move, but her words were indistinct. He turned to look at her, but he couldn't quite make out her features. As if looking through her, he could see the stretch of his fields with small sprouts of wheat waving low to the ground in the high winds.

This isn't right.

The dream always played out this way. Just an instant before he glanced back at the road to see the truck bearing down upon him, he realized that he had to be dreaming. Crucial parts of what had happened that day were missing. Lily's beautiful face, jade eyes, and raven black hair escaped his waking memory; the weather in the dream was always worse than it had been in real life. This time, the overcast sky greyed the long road into town. Victor thought it had been sunny on the day of the accident but couldn't really remember. He dreamed about the accident so frequently that, on particularly bad days, he sometimes confused the dream for reality. Maybe it happened because he spent so much time alone.

"Always the same goddamn dream," Victor muttered to himself, rolling over in bed and trying to fall back to sleep. He knew that the effort was futile. He stayed up for hours after an accident dream. If it was too close to morning, he got up and started his day rather than attempting more shut-eye.

What time is it?

Victor fumbled for his alarm clock radio in the dark and groaned when he saw that it was only four o'clock in the morning. No more sleeping for him tonight, it seemed. He slammed the clock back down on his nightstand and sat up, wearily rubbing his eyes. He reached for the bottle of half-empty whiskey he kept beside his alarm clock and drank deeply before sliding out of bed and fumbling around on the dresser for his painkillers. It occurred to him that he might have better luck finding all of his stuff if he switched on the light, but he didn't want to go to the trouble of searing his eyeballs just so he could find a couple of stupid pills. He finally located the bottle, shook a few into his palm, washed them down with more whiskey, and shuffled out of the bedroom he had once shared with Lily. Miraculously, he evaded tripping over dirty clothes lying on the floor. He missed Lily's housekeeping habits.

Victor stumbled out into the kitchen, then the living area, and then right out the front door, still barefoot. Just before he closed the screen, he heard claws scratching the floor behind him. He waited for Dakota to exit the house with him. These days, the dog was his only companion. Victor traveled to town only for groceries. The only person he saw besides the clerks at Superfoods was his brother, who came to the farm to check on him. No one else came by Nash Farm anymore.

Victor sat on a dusty chair on the front porch and turned himself to the east, preparing to wait for sunrise. He reached underneath the chair and withdrew another whiskey bottle, hesitating only slightly before bringing it to his lips. He felt as though he had something to do today, something that he forgot, something to make it worth staying sober. He tucked whiskey bottles away everywhere in the house. Getting up to find a bottle ruined relaxation and stupor, but something within told him to cool it on the booze today. Why? What was going on?

Victor spent the next several minutes combing his memory for important obligations but failed to remember any. He guessed that he possibly could have a farm chore. He knew that he neglected tasks that he used to do when he was doing a better job at tending to his crops. Nothing came to mind. Harry assumed much of the farm labor now because chronic pain from the accident limited Victor's ability to do the jobs he used to do. He lacked the motivation to do anything except drink. He didn't need human company anymore. Sometimes, even the dog's presence overwhelmed him. He wanted to be alone. Any amount of small talk felt trivial and painful, and Victor felt no urge to connect with anything around him, least of all other people going about life as if nothing had happened. As if he had not lost his soulmate—part of his own soul even.

Victor lingered on his front porch for what felt like hours. When the sun started to rise, he noticed that he felt tired. He heaved himself out of his chair and dragged his body inside the house, almost forgetting Dakota on the porch. He flopped on the couch and closed his eyes, not willing to go through the effort of attempting to get comfortable in bed. He took a long, slow breath, and then...

Someone was hammering on the front door. Victor begrudgingly sat up, blinking at the light illuminating the dingy living room. He didn't feel as though he had slept at all, but clearly, he must have conked out at some point. That, or he could travel through time.

The knocking started up again, and Victor felt a hot flush of annoyance course through his chest.

"I'm coming, I'm coming!" he hollered.

The knocking didn't stop, which more or less told Victor exactly who was on the other side of the door.

That'll be Harry, he thought, peeling himself off of the couch and stomping to the door, kicking up dust from the uncleaned floors. When he pulled it open, he saw his younger brother standing there, looking as annoyed as Victor felt. Harry wore work clothes. Victor knew that the two of them looked a lot alike at one point in their lives. They might again if Victor cleaned up, lost a little weight, and performed more physical labor on the farm. He didn't foresee that happening.

"What, Harry?" he snapped a little more aggressively than he intended. He hated being roused when he actually managed to get some sleep.

"What do you mean, *'what,'* Victor?" Harry threw right back. "You're supposed to be up and dressed and cleaning the house."

Victor opened his mouth to say he had no idea why any of that should be happening. Then, he remembered his feeling that he had forgotten something. The last thing he wanted to do was talk to Harry and cue him into the fact that whatever commitment he made had utterly slipped his mind.

"Sure, okay," Victor said vaguely, "but what are *you* doing here?"

"I'm here for the reason I'm always here. Kick your ass into gear and do some work around here. I know you won't do a thing unless I hound you, so here I am."

"It's a little late to be getting started on fieldwork, don't you think?"

"Coming from someone who used to spend all day wandering around out there? I don't buy it. Besides, that's not what I'm talking about."

Victor stared at him, and after a moment, Harry's lip curled with disgust.

"Goddamn," he said, shaking his head. His eyes never left Victor's. "You don't even remember, do you? You don't remember what today is?"

If he was asking the date, Victor was stumped. If he was asking what was happening today, Victor was equally lost.

"Let me give you a hint," Harry muttered. "Your daughter? Emma?"

Victor shook his head, still drawing a blank.

"She's coming home today, Victor. It's been a year since she lost her mother, and it appears she lost you, too. Emma's coming all this way, and you haven't bothered to throw away these empty bottles?" He kicked an empty whiskey bottle lying by his feet. "The way you live is pathetic. Do you intend to let your daughter see this mess? She's suffering too, you know. The *least* you can do is be strong for her like a father should."

"Have you talked to her?" Victor asked. He knew that he should be in better communication with Emma. He increasingly disliked anyone talking to him when he was in town or bothering him when he was at home, which was most of the time these days.

"Of course, I've talked to her," Harry replied. "How else would I know that she was coming today?"

"*Today?*"

"That's right! I knew that there was no way that you would remember, so here I am, waking you up in your boxers to force you to make this house livable for Emma while she stays here. She told me she was coming today. Do you know why she called me? She worried that you wouldn't be at the train station to pick her up."

"Did she say that?"

"No, but does she have to? Whiskey and pills to numb yourself and run away from reality are all you give a damn about anymore. You don't pay attention to anyone or anything else."

"Stop insulting me in my own house, or leave," Victor said evenly.

"*In* your house? Victor, I'm still standing on the porch, and I see that this place is a mess. It always is. You let yourself and your home and this farm go to hell."

"It's not that bad!" Victor exclaimed.

"Victor, you used to be neat and tidy. Full of strength, always working hard to provide for your family, help the church, build up the community around you. You don't even talk to anyone in town, let alone your own daughter!" Harry huffed but softened his tone a little. "You were always the one who had everything put together, Victor. Perfect wife, perfect daughter, a real pillar of the community, and that's because you were born to be a leader and the guy in charge. You used to take care of everything and were able to fix any problem, Victor. Now you're just a shell of that man. I'm supposed to be the screw-up between us. I know Lily is gone, but you can't just let everything else go to hell."

"Get off my step," Victor growled, "and don't come back. I don't want to see your face around my farm again."

"Hate to break it to you; it's my farm and my livelihood, too.

Since you stopped working, someone has to pick up the slack. I understand your injuries made it difficult at first. Now you choose not to work. Seeing me around here, Victor, keeps the farm going, whether you like it or not. I'd like to see the day we work the land together again."

His heart pounding with fury, Victor slammed the door in his brother's face. Ever since Victor began withdrawing from life and responsibility, Harry sacrificed his carefree lifestyle to keep the farm going. He wasn't about to let Victor forget it, but using Lily as a way of guilting Victor into sobering up and cleaning crossed a line, a line that Victor hadn't previously thought needed to be drawn. It seemed like common courtesy to exclude Lily from their disagreements, but apparently, Victor hadn't been clear enough with Harry. Conversation between the brothers was scarce. Arguing was almost their exclusive form of communication.

Victor resisted the powerful urge to kick something and turned away from the door, surveying his house in the late morning sunlight. A distressing sight met his gaze. Harry had a point. Empty whiskey bottles and discarded medication containers littered the gritty floor. A fine layer of dust coated the furniture and windowsills. It was easy to trace his path around the house: it was the one with the most dirt and the least dust. How could he get the house back in order for Emma's homecoming? What time did her train arrive? He remembered that he stored Emma's letters in his nightstand and made his way to his bedroom.

Victor rifled around in the top drawer of his nightstand. Dakota followed him and sat dutifully beside him, watching intently. Dakota's faithful presence reminded Victor of hunting trips with his brother and the dog in the days before Lily's death. Dakota didn't leave his side then, and it was clear that he still wouldn't.

"Good boy, Dakota," Victor said, giving his dog a rough pat. Finally, he saw the letter that he sought. He withdrew the envelope from the clutter in the drawer, unfolded it, and flipped it over until he was certain he was looking at it right-side up. He read a few sentences about how much Emma was enjoying school and the details of her trip. Sure enough, she planned to arrive today at three o'clock and hoped her dear old Dad would pick her up at the train station.

Victor checked his watch. He needed to clean the house and himself *and then* get his ass to the depot. He asked himself, *Am I sober enough to drive?* Cleaning first, maybe he could wear off some of the booze.

Victor started with the empty whiskey bottles that lay on the floor in nearly every room. He gathered them up in a trash bag and threw them behind the farmhouse, out of sight for the moment. Emma hadn't been home to visit for a year. He felt uncertain about how she would react. Would she scrutinize the house for evidence that he wasn't able to keep things together without her mother? Would she care that he hadn't touched a thing in her room, or would she be glad it was exactly as she left it, albeit dustier? Victor had no way of knowing these things. He decided to quickly clean the most visible surfaces and take a shower before he got in the truck he purchased to replace the one demolished in the accident that took Lily's life.

The afternoon of the accident remained a mystery to Victor until his release from the hospital. One of the county deputies finally informed him that one of his tires blew as he was about to pass the old man who also died in the crash. The randomness of the event and the moment at which it had occurred remained in Victor's consciousness every time he entered a vehicle. After all, what was to stop another blowout from happening today on his way home with his daughter? Would he survive another accident like the first one for which he still blamed himself?

Setting aside his ruminations, Victor grabbed the cobweb-covered broom, which had to be shaken outside before it could be used inside the house. He hurriedly swept the entire house and wiped tables and chairs with a rag to remove dust, the corners and crevices of everything still dirty even when he finished. He cleaned what he could until only an hour before the train arrived. The time had arrived to get himself ready.

Fortunately, showering and shaving took much less time than tidying the house. Before long, Victor loaded Dakota into the back of the truck. Within minutes, he departed the farm to see his daughter for the first time in a year. How much had she changed? Would she notice the changes in him? Had she already sensed he was spiraling into the depths?

There's only one way to find out, I guess, Victor thought to himself as he approached the mouth of the dirt drive leading to the farmhouse. He sighed and carefully turned onto the road that would lead him into town and, ultimately, Emma, the only good thing he had left in his life and the last remains of Lily. Even though they had drifted in the past year due do his grief and addiction, Emma was the only thing in the world Victor cared about. Deep down, he knew she was better off with him at a distance because the father she knew died that day along with her mother.

CHAPTER FOUR

It took Emma a moment to recognize her father when she stepped down from the train. It wasn't just the weight he'd gained, or the lighter tone to his skin, or even the way he carried himself when he got out of the cab of his truck to greet her. It was the look in his eyes and the absence of expression that caught her off-guard. His mouth smiled, but his eyes remained cold and distant, as though all of the happiness within him had been sucked out somehow and replaced with… nothing. Emma brought herself to give him a one-armed hug.

"Hi," Emma said.

Victor just continued to stare at her.

"I said *hi!*" she repeated herself, trying to break the silence between them and bring him out of his trance.

"Oh," Victor's voice cracked, "for a second, you looked just like your mother walking up to me. When did you dye your hair?" His voice seemed shaky and his stare remained distant.

Emma felt a strong sense of shame at the idea that she looked like her mother at all. Not only was she not like her mother, but she was no longer the little girl her mother had been so proud of all those years, either. Trying to claw her way from succumbing to dark thoughts of her questionable decisions, she snipped at Victor, "You might have known already if you bothered to have a working phone."

Dakota, at least, showed genuine happiness to see her. He almost jumped right out of the truck bed to get to her. Emma came to him instead, giving him a good rub while he whined and danced excitedly.

"Looks like he missed you," Victor said, taking the suitcase from Emma's hands and tossing it into the truck bed with Dakota. Opening the passenger's side door of the cab so Emma could climb inside, he added, "Both of us did."

Emma didn't quite believe him but smiled anyway and climbed into the pickup. Something told her that if her father had really missed her so much, he might have bothered to write her more letters or at least get his phone fixed. Speaking of phones, she had called her uncle Harry to come and pick her up today, explicitly asking for him instead of her dad. Irritation burned at her ears at the fact that Victor was the one who came to get her, and that made her feel ungrateful and spoiled.

It's fine that _he's here_, Emma tried to convince herself as they drove down the lane, away from the train station. *I came back to visit him, didn't I?* Somehow, she felt slighted.

The drive to the farm passed in silence. It appeared that neither Emma nor her father had much to say to one another, which made Emma a little sad. It wasn't as though she and her dad had ever been two peas in a pod. She had always been closer to her mother, but after being apart for nearly a year, she thought they would have more to talk about. The truck turned down the dirt road that led to her childhood home, bumping gently along the pocks of potholes from earlier rains. A sense of relief came over her as she finally spied the house rising in the distance. It looked exactly as she remembered it, giving her a little hope for her visit. Maybe the visit wouldn't remain as awkward as it was right now.

Maybe.

Pulling up outside the farmhouse, Victor parked the truck and turned to her, apparently ready to acknowledge her presence.

"You can go ahead and go inside the house," he said. "I'll grab your things."

Emma flushed with fear. She had drugs in her suitcase that she really didn't want her dad to find accidentally, and her bag had a habit of unzipping itself. She needed to handle her luggage herself.

"Oh, it's fine, Dad," she said, hastily jumping out of the cab and moving to the back of the truck before he reached it. "I'll get it. You take care of Dakota."

"If you say so."

The two of them made it to the porch and up the steps without further comment. As she stood outside the front door, Emma surprised herself, anticipating entering her own home and sleeping in her own room again. She knew this house from a different life, but deep down, she knew she was home. When her father opened the door, however, that feeling changed.

The furniture remained the same. Nothing had moved in the home, frozen in time. Despite looking nearly the same, the house was sadder somehow and definitely dirtier. She realized that her dad had *perhaps* made an effort to clean up, but he hadn't done a good job of it. Dust streaked the furniture, counters, and floors. Partially filled whiskey bottles were across the kitchen counter. The smell of liquor permeated the stale air, causing her nose to wrinkle in disgust. She associated the odor with the Phoenix Den, not with her home. Something was terribly wrong.

"What happened to the house, Dad?" she asked, dropping her bag in the middle of the floor. "This place is a mess! Don't you clean at all?"

"Yeah, but things haven't been easy since your mom passed away," he said, not meeting her eyes. Emma could tell that he didn't want to talk about the state of the house, but she wasn't willing to let it go. He had known for months that she was arriving today. Why hadn't he even bothered to pick pill bottles off the floor?

Gee, I sure feel special.

"Things have been hard for me, too, but at least I clean up my apartment when I have people coming over," Emma said, realizing she was being petty, but at that moment, she didn't care.

"I thought you were in college having the time of your life?" her dad retorted, ushering Dakota inside and closing the door behind him. "That doesn't sound too hard to me."

"Of course, it doesn't. You didn't go to college," Emma snapped, folding her arms over her chest. She wore a lightweight long-sleeved shirt to hide the marks on her arms, which suddenly didn't feel like enough to hide herself from view. "You always concentrated on the farm, and that was great. You gave up farming and just did..." she gestured to the room. "...this?"

"Emma, let's not do this," her father said wearily.

Emma blinked. She realized that she was trying to goad him into an argument. Why was she being such a brat? What did she expect to get out of fighting with her last living parent?

An explanation, Emma realized. *I want a reason why Dad thinks he has the right to let this house and farm and his life go to hell.*

Forcing an explanation immediately wasn't worth it. Emma

realized she needed to reconnect with her dad rather than repel him. If she wanted more letters or texts (if he fixed his phone), she knew better that it was necessary to attempt to make this visit less of a living hell for both of them.

"Okay," she said at last. "I'm sorry."

"You've got nothing to apologize for," Victor paused. "How would you like to go and see your mother?"

Emma was caught off guard by her father's question. For several long seconds, she stood mute. Her dad's expression became concerned and understanding.

"I meant her grave," he said quickly.

"I know," Emma assured him. "It just took me by surprise, the way you said it. I... I would like to visit Mom if that's okay with you."

"It's more than okay with me. I visit her a few times a week. I bring her lilies. We can pick some up from the grocery store on the way to the cemetery."

Emma tried to smile through the sense of loss creeping over her. Leaving flowers on her mother's grave after so long would be tough, but it was exactly what she wanted to do.

"Can we go now?"

"Sure. Hop back in the truck."

The duo moved back towards the front door and let themselves outside. Dakota tried to leave with them, but Emma's father blocked the eager dog.

"Sorry, Dakota," he said, "but you're staying back on this one. Cemetery caretakers don't like visitors bringing pets with them."

Once again, father and daughter remained silent on the trip into town. Emma wouldn't have minded some conversation to take her mind off the ordeal to come, but her dad seemed too tense to pay her much attention. Victor's hands gripped the steering wheel, knuckles whitening with the strain, and his mouth reduced to little more than a line on his pale face. Emma watched him out of the corner of her eye as she pulled down the sun visor to look at herself in the mirror. Peering at the image that appeared, she realized that she didn't resemble the girl who had left home months before either. Her hair, once dirty-blonde like her father's, now dyed dark brown, required finger-combing. Smudges under her eyes revealed a hollowed expression. She fussed with her hair, wiped the mascara off with a Kleenex she found in the glove box, and put the visor up again. She returned her gaze to Victor and noticed that he looked more relaxed. They entered the outskirts of town. Whatever caused him to look so alarmed seemed to have passed. Emma almost asked about it, but she kept her observation to herself. Something told her that this was something that her dad wouldn't want to talk about, either.

They parked in the lot at the local grocery store. Victor exited the truck while Emma waited in the car. Her dad rushed into the store and picked up a bouquet of three white lilies, her mother's favorite. With Victor climbing back into the running truck, they remained silent as they continued to the small community cemetery at the edge of town. Emma realized that they were the only visitors today. Maybe it would have been easier on this first visit if other people were around, other people sharing the grief of missing loved ones. *Why didn't I get high before we left? This is a lot harder than I thought it would be.*

"You ready?" her dad asked, jolting her out of her thoughts.

"Yeah," she said, unbuckling her seatbelt. "Let's do this."

Victor led the way through the low, wrought iron gate into the cemetery and made his way down the rows of family gravestones.

Flowers rested at a few headstones, some of them wilted or long ago dead, not yet removed by the graveyard's caretakers. Many of the plots were seemingly abandoned to time, grief forgotten, and names on the stones worn down and difficult to read. How long would it be before her mother's gravestone looked the same?

Clearly, Victor knew precisely where he was going, and Emma felt a sense of shame to discover that she didn't remember exactly where her mother rested. She visited her mother's grave a few times before leaving for college, but it was as though those memories belonged to a different person. She pictured the events after her mother's death and wondered if her family had really changed that much between then and now. Victor had immediately shut down, and it was Harry and others in the community who had taken care of all of the hardest tasks leading up to her mother's funeral. The condolences came in every direction from what felt like a million people but were surely far less in their small rural town, and yet, when was the last time Emma had heard a word from any of those faces, now lost in the haze of drugs and grieving? Had they tried to reach out to her father, and when they did, did Victor shut them out just as he'd been shutting out Emma?

Yes, Emma thought as her father halted in front of a granite gravestone with wilted lilies lying on the grass that covered the plot. *Everything changed. Dad and I changed. The entire world changed.*

Emma took in the sight of her mother's gravestone. *Lillith Glynn, Born February 21...*

Emma watched as her father picked up the sad-looking lilies and replaced them with the fresh ones they brought from the store. He hovered a moment, hunched over the grave, with a grim look as he whispered to himself. Emma had the powerful desire to look away from the intimate exchange between her father and her deceased mom, but Victor suddenly spoke.

"I'll let you have some private time with her," he said, straightening up.

"No, Dad, I don't want—"

"It's fine, Emma. I get to see her all I like, but you don't live here anymore. I'll walk a lap around the cemetery and come right back."

He strode away before Emma could protest, and she was on her own, gazing down at her mother's grave. As much as she appreciated private time with her mother, she felt embarrassed and a little guilty. Did she desert her family by moving away and letting her father fall into the routine of drinking himself to death? She tried to think of something to say to her mom, an apology to offer up, maybe, but she felt at a loss for words. Nothing she could say would be adequate. If her mom was watching her from Heaven, Emma knew that she would be ashamed of how her daughter dealt with her loss. No, her mother didn't judge that way, but Emma knew she would be sad, which might be worse. Sometimes, most of the time, Emma felt sad, too.

Emma's eyes filled with tears as her father returned. She tried to hide her grief, but she knew that Victor saw her smear them away with her thumbs when he approached. Fair to her father or not, Emma felt annoyed that Victor suggested visiting her mother's grave and caught her crying. She wondered if that was his plan from the beginning or if she was just unfortunate. Either way, she felt her heart harden.

"Are you okay, Emma?"

"No, Dad. No, I'm not. Why did you bring me here?"

Taken aback, Victor replied, "I thought that you said you wanted to come and visit your mom."

"No, you asked me if I wanted to come, and I agreed. Why would I want to do this?"

"You haven't seen her in a year. I thought it might be good for you two to catch up."

"Can you stop that?"

"Stop what?"

"Stop acting and talking like she's alive. You do realize she's dead, don't you, Dad?"

"I don't know what you're trying to say, and I don't like your attitude, Emma!"

"It's your fault she's gone!" The tears flowed freely down her cheeks now, and her eyes stung from the rush of tears. She didn't even know where the words she spewed came from or if she believed them, but they poured out of her mouth. "You were driving."

"The tire blew! It was no one's fault, least of all--"

"I can't hear this. I'm leaving!"

Emma turned on her heels and bolted. She ran away from her bewildered father. She ran away from her mother's resting place. Her shoes thudded on the grass. She leaped over graves and tipped over a few bouquets. She wanted to crawl out of her skin and leave the remnants of a life that she didn't identify with anymore. She wanted her mom, not her dad. She sought to escape to the familiar, comforting high that provided the only comfort she had found since she left the farm.

• • •

Victor waited at the cemetery for Emma to return, but she didn't. After a half hour, he left, figuring that she hitch-hiked home. Was he abandoning her? She gave him no choice. What triggered Emma's actions? Perhaps she would have calmed down enough to explain herself once he returned home. It provided a cheerful thought anyway.

The drive back to the farmhouse was short and uneventful. He didn't mind leaving town, but he dreaded driving in the general vicinity of the crash site. Whenever he passed that spot, he experienced losing control of the truck again. Lily's screams rang in his ears as he futilely veered into the other lane and —

Now he was home. It was strange how his brain disengaged like that.

Victor left the truck and entered the house; Dakota greeted him eagerly at the door, tail wagging. He called for Emma through the dark house, but there was no answer. He tried again:

"Emma? Emma?"

Nothing.

Victor sighed, trying not to worry. Emma was old and wise enough to handle herself, but he remained puzzled that she ran away from Lily's grave. Where was she? He thought to himself, *I know things are tense between us, but Emma is all I have left in this world. I can't lose her too.*

Walking down the hall to Emma's bedroom to see if she was there, he noticed the duffle bag sitting in the dingy hallway. He picked it up and carried it to her room, which was indeed empty. As he set it down, the zipper separated in the middle unexpectedly, the contents spilling out onto the floor of her room. Bending down and flipping the suitcase on its back with care, trying to keep what contents hadn't touched the dirty floor clean, he noticed a small baggie.

His heart clenched in his chest as he held the little baggie at eye level and, with horror, gazed at the white powder it held.

No. No way.

Not Emma. Not his beautiful all-American girl. The perfect image and memory he had of his daughter completely went up in flames as he considered her future. Emma, huddled on the street of some nameless city, waiting for her next fix. Was he blowing things out of proportion? After what she did at the cemetery, Victor realized he no longer knew his daughter. He did, however, recognize the feeling of wanting to run away and numb the pain. Victor knew that feeling all too well and knew his daughter had started down the same dark path he was on. Using drugs and booze instead of facing the hard truth that their lives were shattered.

As night fell, Emma still hadn't returned. Victor nursed a bottle of whiskey in the dim light, worrying about her. Just as he considered calling the police, Emma stumbled through the front door. With messy hair and glassy eyes, Emma was clearly drunk. In no position to judge, because he wasn't exactly sober himself, he pulled himself to his feet as his concern voiced itself.

"Where have you been?" he asked, though the answer was obvious enough. Although Emma had never seemed interested in drinking in high school, Victor knew there were always weekend bonfires and house parties. It wouldn't be hard for Emma to find a crowd of old friends willing to share a few drinks from their bottles. Clearly, Emma had found somewhere to drown her sorrows.

"None of your business," Emma slurred.

"You're my kid, and it *is* my business," Victor said, taking a step forward. "You're drunk."

"You're one to talk," Emma snapped. "Leave me alone."

She pushed past him toward her room. Victor didn't try to stop her, knowing she was right to call him out on his hypocrisy. Could he really get on her case for coming home drunk if he was already drunk at home? He was just glad that he'd put her clothes and coke back in her bag. He lacked the strength to face her about that issue tonight. Although, why not tonight? What was there to lose? He didn't want her to think that she slipped drugs past him. He didn't condone illegal drugs. God forbid she turn into another Victor.

Victor marched down the hall after his daughter. Arriving at her room, he saw her flop on the bed, staring at the ceiling. Better to come right out with it, he supposed.

"I know about the coke."

Emma started, surprised to see him standing there, shocked that he knew about the cocaine.

"What?" she asked.

"I know about the coke, Emma," Victor repeated.

"If you're waiting for me to say I'm sorry, I'm not," she said, recovering quickly and replying defensively. Without making eye contact or sitting up, she continued, "You're the one with empty pill bottles sitting all over the living room table. I'm not stupid."

"If you know what a mess I am now, why are you doing such stupid things? You're my smart, beautiful daughter, not this."

"And what is *this*? Huh, Dad? Maybe *this* is just the way I am. You don't know a thing about me anymore. Ever consider that?"

Victor *hadn't* considered that. He knew that it had been a long time since he and Emma were in the same house, but he hadn't expected her to change except to be more mature than the high school girl he hugged farewell the previous year. Suddenly, he comprehended that his perfect daughter might not be so perfect anymore.

Dismissing his daughter's issues for the night, Victor turned from Emma's room and pulled the door shut behind him without another word. *Let her sleep off her drinks while I go back to my own.*

CHAPTER FIVE

When Emma awoke the next morning, she savored the aroma of eggs and toast. For one beautiful moment, she thought it was her mother cooking, but her brain caught up to her heart, and a wave of sadness swept through her. She wondered why her father would cook for her after exchanging harsh words the night before. She decided to return to the city today instead of staying longer. Now that her dad knew about her drug use, she felt exposed. What did he think of her? Did he want her to leave? She wouldn't blame him if he did.

At least he doesn't know about the stripping or dropping out of school, she thought as she sat up and slid out of bed. She ignored her headache, thinking that a little coke would put her right again. So Emma took out her baggie and key and slid it into the bag for a quick bump. Afterward, she supposed she could nibble at her father's breakfast, assuming it was prepared for her. She suddenly realized that he might be making it all for himself.

Emma padded down the hallway and into the kitchen. Even though she moved quietly, Victor looked up at her approach. Scrambled eggs for two, definitely for two, rested on the stove in a skillet. He didn't look good. Like father, like daughter.

"Morning, Emma," he said.

"Good morning."

"How are you feeling?"

Emma tried to figure out if this was a loaded question but decided that even if it was she would answer honestly.

"I've been worse. How are you?"

"About the same, I'd say. Sit down at the table, and I'll bring you eggs and toast?"

That sounded like way too much food for Emma. She had only taken a small bump of coke but she always lost her appetite even after a small hit. But she sat down anyway. She waited until both she and her dad settled down with their plates before she spoke again.

"I'm going to go home today, I think. Can you bring me back to the train station?"

Her father looked surprised, but only for a moment. "If that's what you want to do, I'm happy to take you there. But, Emma, we have to talk about last night."

Emma's heart sank. She wanted to get up and leave but had nowhere to go.

"I see you going down a road that I know well. I can tell you from experience that it isn't a place that you want to go," he went on. "I'm not around anymore to tell you what you can and can't do because you're an adult. I can give you some advice and hope that you take it. I don't… I don't want you to end up a loser like I am now, with no hope, only looking forward to being numb."

Taken aback by his negative comments, Emma wondered why he didn't try to change if he thought he was a loser. She missed her old dad. The steadfast man who stood behind his convictions, cared deeply for her and her mother, and worked hard every day. The dad that she depended on and admired. She wondered if he missed the old Emma.

"Okay. I'll try to do better," Emma said, even though she didn't have any intention of giving up what she was doing. Stripping earned her good money—money that she needed. The drugs helped her to forget what she was doing with her life and the anguish she felt at the loss of her mother, and now her father, and perhaps even herself. She wasn't prepared to give up any of those things just to make her absent dad happy.

"Thank you, Emma."

They passed the rest of breakfast, eating in silence. When Emma finished, she rinsed her dishes in the sink and returned to her room to pack. Her stupor now lessened, and the grogginess out of her head, she truly noticed her room for the first time. Besides the dust, nothing had changed since she left for college the previous year. Photographs of herself and her friends were still taped to the mirror attached to her dresser. Where were those people now? Another photograph of her and her parents during a family camping trip stood slightly askew on the nightstand. Her mother's dark hair rumpled, her father smiling, and her younger self dressed innocently in denim overalls. A rush of memory flooded her, and she felt the urge to leave come on even stronger. To leave the home and to leave her current state of mind.

Emma removed the clothes she had donned the previous morning and shoved them into her duffle bag. Pulling out a clean outfit, she dressed and put her hair up in a ponytail. With the baggie in her hand, she pulled a book from a drawer, dusting it off, before lining up a line of coke that she took into her nostril with a rolled dollar bill. She took in a deep breath, followed by a long sigh of relief. Wiping off the book cover haphazardly and sliding it back into the drawer, she knew it was time to go. She walked back into the main part of the house and found her dad sitting on the couch, staring into space. At least he wasn't drinking yet. Dakota rested by Victor's feet. He rose and thumped his tail when he spotted Emma. Momentarily, she felt happy.

"Can you take me to the station?" she asked.

"Now? You want to go right now?"

"Yeah, if you can take me."

"Let me get dressed, and then I'll take you. I didn't realize you wanted to get to school so early."

Emma almost accidentally told him she didn't know what he was talking about, but she checked her tongue before speaking.

"I have a lot of work to do. Coming here was a mistake."

Her father looked decidedly downcast by this statement, and Emma felt mean, though she didn't know why. Victor didn't care about her. If he did, wouldn't he call or write? Emma resented having to use her uncle as a go-between to obtain news of her own parent.

Fifteen minutes later, father and daughter exited the house. Dakota paced in the truck bed. Emma watched through the rearview mirror and wished she could be so carefree.

Having gone the entire drive in silence, the view of a sparse crowd at the depot waiting to board the train came into view as Victor parked the truck. Emma had timed her departure well, though she hadn't even considered it before leaving the farm. For once, luck favored her.

Emma hopped out of the truck and grabbed her duffle bag from the truck bed before her father could do it for her. She gave Dakota a loving scratch behind the ears and smiled when he leaned into it.

Victor left the driver's door open as he exited the cab. Clearly, he expected this goodbye to be short. He wasn't wrong; Emma had no intention of dragging things out, even though she also secretly relished spending a few extra minutes with her only remaining parent. Maybe the coke was putting her on edge?

Despite being eager to be on her way, she felt a pang of guilt bubbling up inside her chest. She looked at Victor, taking in his hollow expression, and blurted out, "I'm sorry for how I ran off last night. It was…"

Victor cut her off. "It's okay, Emma."

"It's really not, though," she insisted. "I know things haven't been easy for you either, Dad. I am…" she paused. "You're my dad, and I don't want to…"

"You don't have to explain," he said, wrapping his arms around her warmly, Emma returning the gesture in earnest. "I hope you'll be back soon," Victor added.

"I will be," Emma promised, separating from the hug that marked the only real affection they'd given each other during her short trip to Hope River. She had no idea when she would return, but she felt a renewed sense of affinity toward her father. "Bye, Dad."

"Bye, Emma."

Emma smiled at him and began to walk to the depot. She turned back and watched Victor drive away, experiencing an odd mixture of relief and sadness. Even after clashing so much with him for such a short time, it was still sad to see him go.

• • •

NOW ABOARD THE TRAIN, Emma took a seat away from the handful of other passengers. As the train traveled through the Red River Valley and into Minnesota, the droning noises of its movements produced a rhythm that almost felt peaceful as the countryside blurred into colors through the foggy windowpanes. The worn seat and dusty compartment felt oddly relaxing.

Remembering the photograph of her family, Emma's mind drifted to places it hadn't visited in quite some time. She remembered her mother and the family that thrived before Lily died. Coming home from school each day, knowing her mom waited with hugs and cookies. Her mother tutored her when homework seemed too difficult and listened when Emma felt unhappy or anxious. Of course, her dad had always been in the picture, but he busied himself working the farm. Emma spent most of her childhood with, most of her *life* with, her mom. Part of her being died along with Lily. How could she reclaim the happiness that she had known? Could her family recover from the tragedy of losing the glue that held it together? Emma didn't know and felt less than optimistic about the current situation. Maybe a chance, however slight, existed for her to pull herself together, and in doing so, maybe she could help her father get himself together, too.

What could she do, personally, that would help her be a better person? Could she ever be the girl she had been? Maybe she could compromise with herself about going back to school by signing up for online classes. Could she get clean? Imagining making positive changes, though difficult, nurtured some hope that she could accomplish them. She began looking up classes on her phone as the train traveled east, hoping her resolve would hold out.

As the train shuddered to a halt at her destination, squealing brakes brought Emma away from her future and back into the present reality. Although Emma had failed to decide about any specific online courses by the end of the ride, she felt optimistic that she could make a difference in her life with small steps.

Emma exited the station and met Maddie at her white Mustang, riddled with minor dents from the clumsy driving that came with coming down after a shift and driving home tired.

"You don't have any mud on your shoes from the farm, do you?" Maddie asked as Emma opened the door.

"I won't get your car dirty," Emma reassured Maddie as she climbed in. She knew better; Maddie's car might have a few dings, but she liked keeping it clean and free of clutter inside and claimed she'd never need to buy another car.

As they began the drive home, Emma pulled out her baggie of coke and slid the key into it once more, taking a small bump before offering one to Maddie, who accepted and took it easily even while she drove.

"Was it really that stressful?" Maddie laughed but caught herself when she glanced over at a forlorn Emma. "I mean, how was it? Going home."

"It's not really home anymore," Emma sighed. "Well, I guess it is, but my father has stopped cleaning, and it seems like he's usually drunk or high off his pain meds—anything to be numb these days. I don't know. He said I looked like my mother..." Emma paused before mumbling, "I don't really want to talk about it."

Maddie let the silence linger a moment before saying, "That bad, then?"

Emma changed the subject with eagerness in her voice. "I've been thinking I might enroll in some online courses."

"Oh, yeah, that's a good idea. I'm sure you'd do great."

Maddie's supportive words didn't reassure Emma that her

friend believed in her ability to follow through with her goals. Far from feeling encouraged by her friend, Emma still felt energized. She did her best work when she had something to prove. But she knew it was herself she needed to prove something to and not Maddie.

Chapter Six

Saturday night brought with it another shift at the Phoenix Den. Emma wasn't feeling her best, but she dutifully readied herself for her shift alongside Maddie at the apartment they shared. Her mind reverted to school, which motivated her not to get high to get through her shift. She didn't know how she would make it at the Den without being buzzed, but she would manage. She had been through worse, after all.

Maddie and Emma shared the cramped bathroom, the scents of hair products and perfume thick between them. Dancing around each other to use the single mirror over the sink, they attached false eyelashes and painted their lips rosy red. The first few times Emma tried to use fake eyelashes, they stuck to her fingers like melted marshmallow, and she couldn't get the damn things on. Now, she was an expert, barely considering the task as she moved on to the next part of her routine. A touch of black liquid eyeliner elongated the shape of her eyes, a subtle feline effect. Blush warmed her features up, and a bronzer changed the contour of her cheekbones to something slimmer. Her makeup skills transformed her into a different person when she finished preparing herself. For a while, she maintained that her transformation wasn't intentional, just an effort to look pretty. Now, she knew it was easier to do her job pretending that she was someone else. Behind the mask, Emma owed nothing to the world. The persona staring back at her was familiar yet alien to her. It brought confidence in the actions and shielded her from the emotion.

Emma and Maddie finished their nightly routine around the same time, just as they always did when their shifts lined up. They left for work together, at first chatting casually and then falling into silence as club music blared in the cab of the car. Along the way, the street lights against the dark city landscape seemed to twinkle in a way she hadn't seen in a long time. It brought about a feeling of vague nostalgia, an unseen, unheard feeling that sat in her chest. In her mind, she could only explain this nostalgic inkling as a connection to the divine. Inspired by the simple beauty, Emma wanted to attempt another positive change in her life: she was going to reconnect with God.

Emma's relationship with God had always been complicated. The question of the existence of a higher power didn't factor into her childhood beliefs. God simply was, and she believed in Him the same way she believed in the existence of her own parents: implicitly, without question.

"I think I'm going to start going to church again," Emma said aloud, her voice breaking through the bass notes of the music.

Maddie turned the music down. "Why would you want to do that?" she asked, sounding genuinely curious. "I mean, no offense, but we're not really the church-going type."

"I used to be," Emma informed her, "when I lived back home."

This was true. Emma was raised Catholic, and even though her faith had been strongly tested over the past year or so, maybe going back to church would point her in the right direction. When had she last prayed? She wondered if God held grudges.

"Really? I never was, or I might come with you. I would, but, you know, I don't want to." Maddie laughed, and Emma smiled.

"That's fine," she said. "I don't mind going alone. My family used to go all the time, but I guess it's just me now. Honestly, I think it would be weird if we *did* go together."

"How come?"

"I don't know. It just feels like it would be."

"Well, you don't have to worry. I've never set foot in a church, and I don't plan to start now. Do you want a cigarette?"

"Sure, thanks."

"Can you grab them out of my purse?" Maddie requested, keeping her eyes on the road.

"No problem."

As Emma retrieved the smokes, her probing fingers found something much more interesting. Something cold and smooth.

"Maddie, you have a *gun*?"

"You better believe I do," Maddie said proudly. "It's a Derringer. I never go anywhere without it. You should really get one."

"I don't want a gun," Emma said, withdrawing the cigarette pack and trying to keep her hand as far away from the gun as possible.

Maddie shrugged.

"Sure, guns might not be for everyone, but I like the added security. I don't trust people."

Emma guessed that she didn't, either, but she didn't want to shoot anyone. As the two of them sat in the dull droning club music, still turned low, Emma watched her cigarette smoke being sucked out of the open window. She wished that she were like that, light and free. Instead, she felt powerless in her life, as though she were a passenger on a journey that she hadn't elected to start. Maddie had the steering wheel, but Emma was just sitting idly by, watching as her life turned to ash. Except…

"There was one more thing I want to talk to you about," Emma said as they pulled into the Phoenix Den's parking lot and looked for a vacant spot in the rear. Employees weren't allowed to park in the front with the patrons.

"Go for it," Maddie said, killing the engine and turning to face Emma, taking one last draw of her cigarette and flicking it out of her cracked window. "I'm all ears."

"I'm thinking about quitting stripping," Emma admitted, also dropping her light cigarette out of her cracked window before rolling it up.

Maddie looked surprised. "Really? Why? Is it because you're going to try to go back to school? You know that you're going to need the money more than ever if you do something like that, even if you take the classes online like you said."

"No, it's not that," Emma said, though she did take Maddie's words to heart. She hadn't considered this, though she wasn't sure yet if it changed her opinion. "I just want to."

This was about as descriptive as she was able to get. She couldn't explain exactly what was driving her to strive toward making changes in her life. She wasn't happy living the way she was, of course, but that wasn't necessarily the driving force behind her actions. More than anything, even if she could hardly admit it to herself yet, she thought that her dad's words—"I don't want you to end up a loser like me"—had hit home with her. She *didn't* want to end up anything like her dad, that was for sure. But she was already well along that path, and she knew that she had to hop off the bus if she had any chance of salvaging the little that remained of herself. She wasn't sure who she wanted to do it for: her mom, her dad, or herself? Maybe a little of all three.

"Wow, that one-day trip home really changed you," Maddie remarked as they exited the car and walked to the club. Dressed in their street clothes, they would change once they were inside. "Did something happen that made you think all of this stuff?"

Emma wanted to say that the trip home wasn't responsible, but she knew better. Actually, seeing what her dad had become definitely impressed upon her the road she was headed down. She didn't want to reach that destination, and she could already tell the journey wasn't a kind one.

"No, nothing specific," Emma said, deciding to be half-honest. "It was just kind of a wake-up call."

Maddie was too shrewd for non-specifics and too nosy to leave them alone. "Was he in bad shape? Your dad?"

Emma almost didn't answer, but Maddie was one of her closest friends; she knew Emma's story. Maddie knew that Emma's father stopped sending letters and calling. Emma couldn't lie.

"Yeah," she said finally, holding the back door open for Maddie. "He was. He's clearly an alcoholic."

"That's just sad," Maddie sighed. "Not that we're really in a position to judge, I guess."

A part of Emma felt indignant at this, even though it was undoubtedly true. She was getting ready to strip, after all, but at least she was sober. She felt shitty, but she was sober.

Emma worked her shift physically in the Phoenix Den. Nothing new, but this time, she was somewhere different. Usually, she anticipated her next fix and her next drink. Tonight, she imagined a future where she didn't have to do this anymore, which hadn't seemed possible for months. She couldn't believe that she was considering going to church again, perhaps as soon as tomorrow. She couldn't believe that she was motivated to get clean. Could she make it past the end of her shift? At least she hadn't used before work, and that was something. Would God think it was something, too?

The usual existential turmoil of youth assailed Emma in the way it did most teens, but her basic religious beliefs didn't incur any lasting damage in the crises of identity that come with puberty and high school. She had believed God was out there, watching over her family, but when her mother died, Emma's faith shattered as though it had been made of glass. Although taught to turn to God in times of suffering, she felt sure that He must hate her and those she loved when He cruelly stole her mother from her. Something inside her shifted when she saw Victor again. Something made her want to turn back to a Higher Power that she wasn't sure she trusted anymore. She wanted to get to know God again because He might be all she had left.

Emma's shift ended without any customers getting overly grabby, which felt like a good sign. Her reluctant sobriety left her exhausted compared to her nights fueled by cocaine, but she felt in far better spirits than she had in a long time. She wasn't going to wind up as broken and lost as her dad. She wouldn't let herself. Although it was only a small checkpoint on a much longer journey, she knew that tonight's success meant she could accomplish her goals.

Emma's shift ended before Maddie's, and she decided to wait outside by the car for a while and get some fresh air instead of sitting in the stifling back room. She looked up at the sky, washed by the city lights. She couldn't see the stars but knew they were up there.

During times like this, she missed living on the farm, where the night skies were clear and crystalline. When she was a kid, her family used to sit on the front porch of the farmhouse, and her dad would point out the constellations. Emma still didn't know any of them besides Orion and the Big and Little Dippers. Why hadn't she paid more attention?

Maybe I should take an astronomy class.

Emma was still mulling this over when she turned to go inside. She put her hand on the door when her stomach flip-flopped, and she felt a prickle go down her spine. She turned, certain someone was watching her. Her eyes roamed the crowded parking lot. No one stood around their cars, so she took a closer look at the windshields. Just about to give up, she saw that a man *was* sitting at the wheel of a car and staring at her. He was nothing more than a silhouette, but Emma could feel his eyes on her. Emma's eyes widened, and she hurried inside the Phoenix Den, where she felt comparatively safe. April, another stripper, was touching up her makeup in the dressing room when Emma entered, and she looked up in surprise.

"Emma? Are you okay?"

Emma caught sight of her reflection in the mirror and saw that she looked just as alarmed as she felt.

"I… I'm fine," she stammered.

"Girl, you are not fine. Just tell me what happened."

"Someone is sitting in a car and staring at me," Emma explained. "It sounds stupid when I say it out loud."

"No way! That's super creepy," April exclaimed, putting away her lipstick. She looked ticked. "Show me where he is. I'll go and teach him a lesson."

Emma laughed a little, feeling calmer with the generosity of

April's response and nonchalant attitude.

"That's not necessary," she said. "Seriously. I'm fine."

"Are you sure? Because I'll go out there and beat the shit out of him. I took self-defense when I was a Girl Scout."

Emma nodded, smiling. She already felt better. She figured that she had overreacted. For all she knew, that guy, or maybe even a girl, was on the phone or waiting for a friend. In fact, she didn't know for sure that the person in the car had even been looking at her. She *imagined* that they had been, but she couldn't actually see anyone's eyes on her.

I'm just making a big deal out of nothing, she decided.

April went back to work, and after a while, Emma went back outside, mostly to reassure herself. The car had left, though she shouldn't have been surprised. It was probably just an old, middle-aged man trying to escape his monotonous marriage for a few hours like most of the Den's customers. Sighing at herself, Emma returned to the Phoenix Den again, deciding to wait for Maddie inside. Whether someone had been watching her or not, it was definitely better to be on the safe side.

Chapter Seven

Emma woke up early to attend church the following morning, just as she had promised herself. To her surprise, Maddie was already awake and wearily making coffee.

"What are you doing up so early?" Maddie asked groggily.

"I'm going to church," Emma reminded her.

Maddie snorted, "You were serious about that?"

"Yes!" Emma found herself feeling a little hurt and defensive. "I'm really going. I want to fix my life and have goals and a better future for myself beyond dancing and drugs. I feel like this is a good first step. Do you want to come?"

"No, thanks," Maddie said as though the question were the most ridiculous thing she had heard in a while. "I'll sit this one out."

Emma didn't press her; the last thing she needed was to have someone talk her out of going to church since she already felt more than a little shaky about it. She tried to picture what returning to God might be like. Would she feel the crushing weight of all of her sins on her shoulders? Would relief come with her return to worship? Probably, the answer lay somewhere in the middle. Even so, she felt nervous. Laying there awake, it had taken her a while to leave her bed this morning and then even longer to muster the courage to get in the car. She was glad she woke up early; if she hadn't, she would have been walking into church late.

Emma knew exactly where the Catholic church—Our Lady of Perpetual Grace—she wanted to attend was located. The drive to church felt long, even though the actual distance was short. By the time she pulled into the church parking lot, she had worked up a fair amount of trepidation and sat in her car for several long minutes. Her hands rested on the steering wheel as her brain worked. The urge to leave dominated her thoughts, but Emma knew she needed to give this a shot. If there were any hope of getting her life on track, it would start here with God.

Emma finally pulled the keys from the ignition and put them in her purse. Taking a deep breath, she let herself out of the car, locked it, and began her walk to the sanctuary. Her low heels clacked on the asphalt. Emma's shoes were the plainest she owned, but they were probably still a bit much for church. She didn't own any flats, and she didn't want to wear sneakers. Heels were the best she could do, and this was her only pair that didn't quite scream "stripper," even if they maybe still suggested it. She pictured people staring at her and fought the urge to leave once more, but instead of returning to the car and driving away, she forced herself to keep walking.

Moving slowly, she took in the sight of a few people near the doors talking to each other, well dressed in their Sunday best, and smiling at one another. Would these people someday become the company she kept instead of the perfume-laden, scantily clad strippers she associated with now? By the time her baby steps brought her to the front of the church, the small group had already ventured inside. She stood there alone, looking at the massive oak door looming before her. It felt like a tapestry in time with its ornate carvings of religious imagery, which felt simultaneously familiar and somehow new to her. A sense of panic crept into her chest as she reached for the handle, but she opened it anyway.

Instead of relief, the interior of the church gave Emma the chills, but not because it was creepy. The high ceilings and kaleidoscope stained glass windows reminded her of the beautiful and ornate church she attended with her family back home. Her family had sat together in pews nearly every week for years, enjoying their Sundays together. She knew now that she had taken those precious moments for granted as a child. As the scents of incense and old wood filled her nostrils, she longed for the return of that version of herself, her family, her life. Perhaps, with luck, this was the first step in getting to the next best thing.

Emma found a pew near the back and sat alone as the sanctuary gradually filled. She knew it was a good time to kneel and talk a little one-on-one with God. What could she talk to Him about? She didn't fear God's wrath, but, at the very least, she knew she had disappointed him. Could she navigate a reconciliation with the Lord?

Taking in the light streaming through the stained glass, creating a burst of color across the room, the imagery of the crucifixion burned at her a bit, but she focused instead on the white dove flying above His head. Emma hadn't strayed from her faith so much that she didn't realize the solution to understanding her feelings and regaining the respect of her loved ones remained locked inside her. The dove's presence in the beautiful glass all but promised rebirth, but she couldn't find quite the key despite the message of hope before her.

The pews filled quicker now, and soon, the service began. People sat beside Emma in her pew. As the congregation stood, knelt, and prayed, she wondered what they thought of her. What did the priest think? Could these people look at her and know her sins? Did she *look* like a stripper? Were any of them as lost as she was, coming here for guidance and a connection to God? Or were they merely maintaining their already-earned righteousness, reveling in their worship instead of their sin? She couldn't receive the Sacraments because she hadn't yet gone to confession. Were the congregation and the priest wondering why she didn't go forward to receive the Host? How could she confess? Was there that much time?

In a blur of detached emotion, the mass ended too soon. Emma stood for a moment, eying the congregation as they streamed out of the pews and down the aisle toward the double doors of the entrance. She wasn't sure what she hoped to gain by attending church, but she didn't feel as though she had gotten much out of it. She didn't feel closer to God, and she didn't feel cleansed of all of the nasty things she had done since leaving home. It was unreasonable to expect just one hour of church to do all that, she supposed, but she longed to leave the building feeling better about herself and her life than when she entered.

Emma sighed and moved towards the main aisle, meaning to join the exodus heading towards the door in a low rumble of friendly conversation. However, she stopped when a thought popped into her head: *Should I go to confession now?*

In truth, it had been years since she confessed. Even when she attended church regularly with her parents, she usually skipped confession, although she told her parents otherwise. How many sins did a high school kid have to confess? Back then, her religious incentive was going out to breakfast with her family after the mass ended. Nobody waited to take her out to eat now. Emma's adult self realized that her sins were many and required forgiveness.

I'm doing it.

Emma waited until the flow of people slowed down enough for her to squeeze in and walk toward the confessional. A few people waited as Emma joined the line of repentant sinners. She was alone in her thoughts as one after another went inside, closed the curtain, and returned with their penance. Some of them took a while, but others were quick. Emma hoped that she would be totally honest about her life instead of keeping the worst bits and pieces festering within her.

As she stood there, Emma felt an unexpected, curious prickling run up her neck.

Someone's looking at me.

She glanced around and saw a man near the doors on the opposite side of the church. He stood apart from the people still trickling outside. Distance prevented Emma from seeing many details of his appearance, but he was tall and had black hair, brown eyes, and a dark complexion. Why was she feeling nervous?

Emma's job taught her to trust her gut feelings. If someone felt like a creep, they probably were. It was not like she could do much of anything from where she stood. Besides, it was almost her turn to go and talk to the priest. Safely out of sight in the confessional, she wouldn't have to worry about the guy anymore.

Emma's turn to confess her sins arrived. Could she make an honest confession? She would try. Entering the confessional's cramped interior, hardly breathing, she willed her heart to slow its pace as she drew the curtain closed. Thoughts raced through her mind. Would she be welcomed when the priest heard about her sins?

In an abstract way, she realized there was nowhere else to turn. Maybe her Uncle Harry was approachable, but he wasn't there. Without the mercy she sought, her depression would overwhelm her.

Don't think about that. Just focus on what's happening now.

"Bless me, Father, for I have sinned," she said, trying to keep the tremor out of her voice. "It has been... a long time since my last confession. I accuse myself of the following sins."

She waited, catching her breath and trying to see through the screen to her left out of the corner of her eye.

"Go on, my child," the priest prompted. His kind voice eased Emma's hesitance. She took a deep breath and launched into her story, keeping it as brief as she could. The priest didn't interrupt her with questions or tell her that she was taking too long. No accusations assailed her soul. She finished, and her soul felt lighter and much more certain that she could begin a new chapter in her life. Dumping all the negatives—the booze, the drugs, the stripping, the mindless sex, all things she did that convinced her she was worthless—she asked herself whether she had the strength to undo those old habits. Didn't she have the strength?

"For these sins and all those that I cannot remember, I humbly repent and ask for absolution, counsel, and penance," Emma said once the verbal recounting of her sins ended. She thought of the people still standing outside the confessional. She wondered if they were growing impatient with her. If they were, it didn't matter. If keeping her fellow sinners lingering while she cleansed her soul was the price of forgiveness, she would ignore the glares of those who were waiting when she exited the booth.

"Thank you, my child," the priest said. "You have been through a lot over the past year, but your soul is not lost. Say eight Hail Marys and keep coming to church. It will help you feel better and get your life back on track."

"Thank you, Father."

Emma got up and tentatively left the confessional, almost afraid to walk back into the light of the outside world. It felt so safe in there, laying out her life to someone who would not judge her, no matter what she said. Outside of the booth, she returned to being a stripper and a druggie who was only thinking about getting clean. She didn't want to be herself, but there were few other options. In fact, there weren't any at all. She would have to be herself and herself alone for the rest of her life, and she didn't like how that made her feel. She tried to shake it as she knelt in a pew close to the confessional and recited her Hail Marys, concentrating on her penance.

Through the concentration of her prayers, Emma sensed someone watching her. She snatched a quick glance at the back of the church and noted the same man watching her. Her heart skipped a beat. She turned back to face the altar and felt her clasped hands starting to shake. She tried to resume praying, but her mind focused on the internal voice screaming that the man still watched her. Why? Was he mistaking her for someone else? She doubted it. She met plenty of creeps at work, and she had a strong sense that he was one of them.

Emma forced herself to finish her penance and then got up, looking around to locate an alternative exit. To her immense relief, she spotted a side door and exited hastily.

She pondered her return to worship and decided it was a positive experience. She felt like a stranger to her faith, but she realized that would disappear with time. She had never tried to find a new church before, and she supposed that everyone must feel displaced when they had to do so.

Emma walked around the building to the parking lot in front of the main entrance, searching for her car. She found it and was well on her way toward it when the same sensation of being watched washed over her again. Her stomach twisted. She fought the urge to glance over her shoulder, but something instinctual told her not to.

Pretend you don't know. Ignore the surroundings.

Emma trusted her instincts and continued walking toward her car at what she hoped resembled a normal pace. Reaching the driver's door, she allowed herself a stolen glance over her shoulder and saw… nothing.

That's weird, Emma thought, frowning. *I could swear…*

Maybe her anxiety was getting the better of her? Maybe the effort to stay sober strained her nerves and made her overly anxious? Or, maybe someone was watching her, and if so, where was he now? How could she be sure that the man hadn't followed her here? What if he concealed himself behind a car, waiting for her to let down her guard?

"You're *really* paranoid," Emma told herself aloud, opening the car door. Just because one person looked in her direction a couple of times, it didn't mean that he was a stalker who endangered her life. Strippers and exotic dancers learned the hard lesson of not trusting anyone without an understanding of their motives. Was it all in her head? Why would a random man be observing her so closely?

Emma buckled her seatbelt and joined the line of cars still leaving the parking lot. She stared at the church in the vehicle's rearview mirror. She attempted to convince herself that it was a casual glance. Emma relished the rekindling of her faith, but a tiny part of her waited for that man to come out so she could take one more look at him. He failed to appear as Emma left the church, the thoughts of a potential stalker fading as she drove away.

CHAPTER EIGHT

The following Saturday brought with it another shift at the Phoenix Den, this time without Maddie. As Emma prepared for her day, a bouncer, who worked even more hours than she did, approached.

"Hey, Emma," he said, summoning her over from where she was dancing.

"Hey, Kyle," she smiled.

"You've been requested for a private dance."

"Really?" Emma said, jumping down from her platform and frowning. She hated doing private dances. It was difficult to pretend that she was another person in a different line of work when she danced for someone one-on-one.

"Really," the bouncer said. "He's waiting on you. Follow me."

Emma obediently followed him around tables, occupied mainly by men. She noticed only a few women scattered here and there in the shadowy establishment. The private rooms were attached to the back of the club, shielding the customers from the public gazes of others and promising something more intimate yet not truly intimate at all. Emma strutted toward them with all the bravado she could muster. Men disliked half-hearted lap dances. Her feelings mattered to no one; money was the concern. Emma determined that she would keep her mind on that instead of thinking of a recent preoccupation: her stalker.

She had tried many times to put it out of her mind, but okay, maybe she had a stalker. Her gut told her she was being watched when venturing out alone despite her only sighting occurring at mass the previous week. She considered taking Maddie's advice and buying a gun for her purse. Just a little one, nothing too scary. Maddie loaned Emma her car for her current shift, so, fortunately, she wouldn't have to hoof it home this time. Sometimes, a long walk after a shift was welcome, but given her current paranoia, that was definitely not the case lately.

The bouncer directed Emma down a hallway lined with curtains and stopped before one near the end. He pulled the curtain back and gestured for Emma to enter.

"After you," he said expressionlessly.

Emma took a deep breath, pasted what she hoped was a sultry smile onto her face, and sashayed into the room. The small room contained a leather bench for the patron to sit on while she showed off her assets. Her smile faltered a little when she saw who was sitting there, a dark-skinned black man. Did he look familiar? Who could tell in the murky mood lighting? Emma steeled herself and strutted to face her customer.

"Hey, handsome," she breathed, settling herself in his lap. "I hear you want a dance. You sure you can handle me?"

"I'm game to find out, baby," the man replied smoothly, not missing a beat. As was common at the Phoenix, his looks failed to impress, but male models didn't pay girls to pay attention to them.

The music from just down the hall reached the private dance room, and Emma twisted sensuously to the beat. Her mind a million miles away, she prepared to release the string holding up her top, then halted, realizing that her customer had spoken.

"What was that, honey?" she asked, remaining in character.

"I asked where you're from," the man repeated more loudly.

"California," Emma replied, leaning forward and letting her top drift to the floor. She always lied when people tried to make small talk with her on the job. Not only did it increase the distance between herself and her job, but she sounded sexier and, therefore, might end the evening with more cash. Being a California girl sounded much hotter than being a farmer's daughter from North Dakota. Danger came with providing too much personal information, anyway, and her personal life was hers alone. Exposing her breasts didn't mean she was required to expose her soul. Money couldn't buy who she was deep down underneath everything she had become… not yet, at least.

"California, huh?" the man said. "That's nice. Where in California?"

"L.A."

"I've got a cousin in L.A."

"Wow!" Emma said, trying to sound fascinated and sexy at the same time. She thought that she succeeded because the man reached out when she left his lap and touched her ass as she was shaking it in his face. She backed away and wagged a finger, refusing to break character. "No touching!" she chided.

"It's hard to resist."

"You like what you see?" Emma cooed, continuing her dance. Although sickened by the experience, she felt she hid it well. Inquisitive, talkative customers made her question whether her lies were transparent. Was she as good an actress as she thought?

"You bet I like," the man replied, his eyes roaming over her exposed body. "You're a beautiful young lady. What's your name?"

"I'm Jade," Emma replied huskily. She always used that name at work, and customers requested her by that name. Why ask when he already knew?

"Well, Jade, how would you like to come home to a real man every night?"

"*Ooooooh*, nice!" Emma squealed. Creeped out by his line of questioning, she decided that the dance was over. "Okay, sweetie. If you want more, you need to pay a little more."

"More money? I'm a gravedigger," the man informed her. "I don't have extra cash. I came here to see you, Emma. I knew that this might be the only way I could connect with you."

Emma's stomach dropped, and she hurried to grab her top off the floor.

"Kyle!" she called. The bouncer pulled back the curtain at once and entered the room.

"Something the matter in here?"

Emma scoured her mind to find a reason to eject the chatty customer.

"He's tight with his cash," she said, slipping her top back on and tying it behind her neck.

"I can pay you in more than money," the man said, getting to his feet as though he were gearing up for a fight. His dark eyes, however, were locked on Emma's. "Stay a little longer, or come home with me."

"He's being a creep," Emma said, looking to Kyle, the bouncer, for help.

"Okay, buddy," Kyle said, stepping forward. "No more money,

no more private dance. It's as simple as that."

"Come on, Emma," the man begged. "Don't be a stick in the mud."

"Please, get him out of here," Emma said, folding her arms over her chest. The man's eyes kept straying to her breasts, and she wished that she hadn't exposed herself to him. On this job, random weirdoes wanted to take things too far, but no one called her by name. She wondered how he had learned it and how much more he knew about her. Did he know that she was lying about being from California? Did he know where she lived *now*?

"You can't get rid of me that easily," the gravedigger said, visibly irritated. "Why won't you let me talk to you? Hey!" he exclaimed as Kyle grabbed him by the arm. He jerked away. "Don't touch me!"

"You're out of here, pal," Kyle commanded, grabbing both the gravedigger's hands behind his back and forcing him from the room. The customer continued to protest, but Kyle was bigger, and any attempts to resist were futile.

Emma stood in place for a minute, trying to lower her heart rate as she did her best to absorb everything that had transpired over the last few minutes. The escalation from a routine lap dance to an invasion of privacy frightened her badly. The whole encounter played over and over in her mind rapidly. She frowned as she recalled her initial suspicion that the man looked familiar. Focusing as she calmed herself, she thought carefully. Familiar faces at the Phoenix were common because satisfied customers became repeat customers. There were lots of repeat patrons at the Phoenix Den. Maybe he was merely an established customer who decided to treat himself to a lap dance.

Okay, but how did he know my real name? Emma wondered, racking her brain for an answer that wasn't freaky and coming up with none. Did she have a stalker? Was she being paranoid, jumping to conclusions? How could the gravedigger *really* know her true identity? Had she accidentally mentioned her real name at some point in the evening, and he overheard? Had she met him outside of work? Why did he have to remember her?

Sighing to herself, Emma returned to work. Seeing no sign of her creepy customer among the club patrons, she surmised that Kyle succeeded in ejecting him. Even though she was completely safe in the Phoenix, Emma remained distinctly on edge through the remainder of her shift, though she concealed it. She thought about the little gun hidden in Maddie's purse and finally fully understood. She would definitely feel more confident carrying a firearm.

Emma's evening finally ended and early morning arrived as she changed into her street clothes by the back-room lockers. Generous tips made her feel good about her shift despite the earlier fright. She still intended to quit stripping, but she would miss the money, for sure. Could she find another job with the same income, maybe at a Hooter's? She heard tips there were good.

Way to shoot for the stars, Emma, she thought. She finished tying her shoes, and chills raced through her body as she approached the door to leave.

What if he's out there waiting for me? a scared little part of her wondered. This part of her that viewed too many horror movies and true crime shows couldn't be easily silenced. She considered her options for a moment, then decided to go and ask the outside bouncers to walk her to her car. She would feel better with protection for the short walk.

Easing cautiously into the night, Emma made a beeline for the security guards, Pipes and Zach, standing nearby, chatting casually while April smoked by herself. They noticed her just before she reached them and stopped their conversation, clearly anticipating some problem. Emma tried to look casual, but she failed. An overwhelming desire to safely reach the car and drive home urged her forward.

"Everything okay?" Zach asked.

"I... yes and no," Emma said unhelpfully. "Please walk me to my car? A creep harassed me earlier, and I'm scared that he might still be out here."

"Yeah, I heard about that," Pipes added. "I haven't seen anyone lurking around here, though."

"Still, I would feel a lot more comfortable if I didn't have to go to my car alone," Emma insisted.

Pipes glanced at April, who was obliviously smoking her cigarette. Zach, apparently reading his counterpart's mind, stepped up to the job.

"I'll take her," he said. "You can stay here and keep April company."

"Alright."

"Come on, Emma. Where's your car?"

Emma led him to the rear parking lot, feeling grateful for the added protection. She found Maddie's car and unlocked it from a distance, the headlights flashing. Zach waited until she quickly placed herself in the driver's seat and bid her goodnight as he returned to his spot outside the club. The radio blared loudly when Emma started the car, so she lowered the volume as she pulled out of the parking lot and drove home. As she drove, she smoked a cigarette and tried to relax. Because the drive was a familiar one, she allowed her mind to wander, half-listening to the radio. Her thoughts ventured to another place and time when her family remained intact and she wasn't a stripper trying not to get high.

• • •

WHAT EMMA *DIDN'T* KNOW was that Ed Crane, the gravedigger, was in her backseat. She unwittingly neglected to lock her car upon starting her shift. She hadn't thought to look in the rear of the car before entering. Ejected by the bouncer, Ed had easily slinked through the parking lot and gained entrance to the car to lay in wait as she drove home.

Emma pulled into her parking space back at the apartment complex that Ed already knew she called home. He waited until she killed the engine, the radio stopping abruptly, before he sprung forward with a rag soaked in chloroform, covering her nose and mouth from around the driver's seat. Emma screamed and thrashed, scratching at his arms as she did. She almost broke free from Ed's grasp, but her strength diminished as she succumbed to the chemicals. Emma lost consciousness and slumped against the window, held in place by the seat belt she hadn't had time to unbuckle yet.

Finally ascertaining that Emma wasn't going anywhere, Ed slipped out of the backseat and opened the driver's door, supporting Emma as he released the seatbelt. He glanced around for witnesses before dragging her out and placing her in the backseat where he had crouched minutes before. With his victim stowed, he entered the car, sat down behind the steering wheel, started the engine, and drove Emma away into the night.

CHAPTER NINE

When Emma didn't come home from the Phoenix Den the previous night, Maddie assumed she had been called in for a double shift. She went to bed, assuming she would see Emma in the morning. However, when she woke up and saw Emma's bed undisturbed, she felt a tinge of worry creeping in. She searched the apartment, half-expecting to find Emma passed out on the couch. It wouldn't be the first time. Seeing no sign that Emma had even made it home, Maddie went outside to see if the car was in their allotted space, but it stood empty. Shaken, Maddie smoked a cigarette as she dialed Emma's number three times, going to voicemail each time. Continuing to stare at the vacant parking spot as though she might be able to bring Emma back with sheer will-power, she finished her cigarette before attempting one more call. After getting voicemail again, Maddie decided it might be time to call the police station.

"My roommate is missing," Maddie blurted into the phone. "Her name is Emma Nash, and she didn't come home last night from work."

The woman on the other end was deadpan in her delivery: "Ma'am, please calm down. You said she didn't come home from work last night? If it's only been a few hours, she's probably just out still. Someone being gone for a few hours isn't a missing person."

Maddie explained the situation, giving the operator information that was asked from her, including where Emma worked, that she'd borrowed Maddie's car, and even that she felt as though she'd been watched recently. The operator kept repeating that she should just wait longer for her friend to show up before making it into a police matter. "Adults can come and go as they like, and *someone like her* is probably just out trying to get high."

Maddie knew what "someone like her" meant: "a worthless stripper drug addict." Despite continually trying to push the issue, Maddie received several more heartless responses from the operator on the other line finally spelling it out. "Look, strippers run off all the time and show up in a few days after a bender. I wouldn't be surprised if she just took your car for a joyride to find someone she can blow for a fix to keep the party going. I'll mark your car as missing, but otherwise…"

Maddie didn't bother listening to the rest and just hung up. Emma might have her problems, but she always called if she would be late, and she would never take advantage of having borrowed Maddie's car. Emma was kind of a bottom-feeder—and, hey, so was Maddie, so no judgment—but even Emma cared enough to call if she was going to be late returning Maddie's car. Something was wrong. There was no way around it. But what could Maddie do?

Trying to remain calm, Maddie walked to a nearby diner to pick up some breakfast as she contemplated what to do next. Redialing Emma's cell phone and leaving several texts had done nothing to change the situation. She hoped to find Emma in the home when she returned, but the car was still gone, and entering the apartment, she found it completely unchanged. Maddie placed her grease-soaked breakfast bag on the counter while she hunted around the apartment, seeking out a phone number to lead her to her friend. Emma's dad didn't have a phone anymore; that's why she always wrote him letters. Still, there had to be someone in Emma's family to help Maddie in her search.

That search failed, however. Choosing to go a different route, Maddie decided to check at work to see if she had mentioned going somewhere to her co-workers the last time she worked. As she walked to the club, she practiced what she would say. First, she would ask if anyone saw Emma and when. Then, she would ask if they talked to her. Next, she would ask if anyone knew where she might have headed after her shift. Maddie opted to be discreet and casual in her questions to protect Emma's privacy. *Easy, peasy.*

Maddie began with the bouncers at the front door, who had familiar faces, although she didn't know their names. These two worked primarily during the day. Maddie and Emma, being young and beautiful, were not daytime strippers. "Hey, sorry to bother you, guys, but have you seen Emma?" she asked.

Both frowned at her, and she realized they didn't know the night shift staff. To them, Maddie was a complete stranger asking for another complete stranger. This wasn't going to work.

"Who?" the bigger of the two asked, but Maddie shook her head.

"Never mind," she said. "I'll look for her myself."

Though completely the same, the club's interior somehow appeared more depressing during the daylight. Surprisingly, people filled some of the chairs. People who belonged at work instead of watching somebody's mom stripping during the school day for extra cash to pay bills. Pretty depressing.

Maddie glanced around the club and recognized a girl she

knew who sometimes worked night shifts. *What was her name? Bella?*

What's her real *name?* Maddie wondered, already walking towards her. It didn't matter, she supposed; "Bella" probably wouldn't want the people in here knowing her real name, anyway.

"Hey, Bella, can I talk to you really quick?"

"Wait your turn, dyke," a man sitting at the table in front of her snapped.

Annoyed, Maddie snapped back, "*Excuse* me?"

"Just a second, baby," Bella said, giving her guest a sultry smile. Turning her back on the irritated customer, Bella's expression immediately changed to one of annoyance. "What are you doing? In case you didn't notice, I'm working here."

"It will only take a second," Maddie said quickly. "Have you seen Emma?"

"Who?"

"She goes by 'Jade' here? Dark hair? Works nights?"

"I don't know no Jade." She shrugged. "Sorry, I'm busy with this guy who's paying me to give a damn now."

She turned her back on Maddie, effectively dismissing her. Maddie didn't like that but reined in her temper and forced herself to focus on her mission.

I'm looking for Emma, she thought, scanning the club for someone who might have a clue as to where she had gone. *Just think about Emma.*

This was the wrong time to be looking for her roommate in this place. Day customers and night customers were different groups. It was stupid to come here in the middle of the day. *Think, Maddie, think.* Turning to leave, fuming at herself for walking all the way to the club for nothing, she spied a familiar face. Kyle, the bouncer, was standing in a back corner of the room with his arms folded over his chest as he surveyed the room before him. Would he have a clue about Emma's plans from the previous evening?

"Kyle!" Maddie said loudly to be heard over the music. She crossed the room as he looked around to see who had called his name, and after a few seconds, his eyes locked on hers.

"Hi," he said once she stood before him. "What's up?"

Maddie could tell from the tone of his voice that he didn't really care, so she cut to the chase.

"Emma's missing. Have you seen her?"

"Who?"

"Jade," Maddie clarified, rolling her eyes.

"Not since last night," he said apathetically.

Disgusted with his attitude, Maddie pressed him. "Okay, well, she never came home. Did you see anything weird last night?"

"Like what?"

"I don't know!" Maddie exclaimed, exasperated. "Did you see anyone stalking her or anything?"

Something in Kyle's expression changed, and Maddie realized that she jogged his memory. She felt a thrill of anticipation.

"Yeah, actually, now that you mention it," he said slowly, "one of the bouncers had to throw someone out. He paid for a private dance but got too handsy."

"Can you describe him to me?"

Kyle's brow creased with annoyance.

"What's with the third degree? Is she missing or something?"

"Yes, she is. I told you already that she didn't come home last night. I'm trying to find her. What did the guy look like?"

"Jesus, I don't know! Just a regular-looking dude. A million and one guys who come in here just like him."

"That's not super helpful."

"I'm not here to help you play detective," Kyle snapped. "I'm here doing my job! She's probably out getting high. Get out of my face."

Maddie bristled, "You can't talk to me like that."

"I can. Get out before I throw you out," Kyle sneered.

Maddie turned around without further prompting, but as she walked away, she heard Kyle mutter just loudly enough for her ears to pick up:

"Dumb whore."

Her blood instantly filled with white-hot rage, but she didn't turn back. Maddie stomped out of the Phoenix Den. She fumed all the way home, but when she reached the apartment, her mind was back on Emma. The trip to the strip club wasn't a complete waste. She learned that someone drooled over Emma and was rejected and ejected. That sounded pretty suspicious to her, even if it wasn't exactly unheard of in their line of work.

If only Kyle wasn't such a moron and could remember what the guy really looked like. Frustrated, Maddie opted to seriously rip Emma's room apart in search of clues. She had dug around for a number earlier but hadn't truly invaded Emma's privacy. She realized that this might be her last chance to help before she had to get a ride to the police station and beg them for the help they denied her over the phone. Instead of casually poking around, she'd continue until she found a clue.

Dumping everything out of Emma's nightstand drawer, Maddie finally located something that made her heart skip a beat: a scrap of paper with "Uncle Harry" scrawled at the top and a phone number underneath. She stood with her cell phone clasped in her hand, trying to gather the courage to dial the number. Maddie wasn't as scared to talk to "Uncle Harry" as she feared what she might learn when she did. If Emma wasn't there, then it was time to reach out to the police again and force them to take her seriously.

Trying first to dial Emma's number one last time to no avail, Maddie took a deep, steadying breath and dialed the number on the paper slowly, ensuring she got the numbers correct. She wasn't in the mood to misdial and lengthen this process. Emma could be in trouble. The phone rang a few times, and finally, somebody picked up:

"Hello?"

"Hi, is this… Harry?"

"Yes. Who's asking?"

"My name is Maddie," Maddie said quickly. She didn't want to get hung up on, so she had to get this out quickly. "I'm a friend of Emma's? Have you seen her?"

There was a pause.

"What do you mean?" he inquired. The question seemed genuine. "Did she come home to the farm again?"

"I'm not sure," Maddie fretted. "I'm her roommate, and she hasn't come home since she went to work last night. I'm really worried."

"I don't blame you," Harry said. He sounded concerned himself. "Unfortunately, I haven't seen her, either. I like to think that if she was in town, she would have visited me, but, well, you never know. I can go see her dad and ask if she's back again. Her last stay was really short, but I'm sure you already knew that."

"Yeah, she only left for a day. But, when she left that time, she told me where she was going, and she brought a bunch of her stuff with her. This time, everything's still here, *and* she took my car."

"Well, Maddie, I understand your distress. Have you called the police?"

"I tried this morning," Maddie sighed, "but they didn't care." Maddie explained the disinterested interaction she had with the police earlier in the day, leaving out some details about Emma's whereabouts and profession.

"That's not good. I think you should try them again soon." There was another moment of silence while Harry thought. "The only thing I can think to do here is head over to my brother's place and see if she's there. It sounds unlikely, but it's worth taking a look. It was good of you to call me, Maddie. I don't know how you got this number, but I'm glad you did. I'll let you know if I find anything."

"Me, too."

Maddie already felt a little better. Her next step would be to call the cops again. The emotional load of Emma's disappearance transferred from her shoulders to Harry's. Harry and Emma's dad could look for Emma, and Maddie could stop running around trying to find her car-stealing friend. She needed another cigarette to calm down. Everything was probably fine. Maybe Emma had a sudden urge to go home to see her dad. She hoped that Harry would call her back with good news.

• • •

VICTOR WOKE RELUCTANTLY to Dakota's barking. He spotted a familiar car pulling up the drive, kicking up dust, and realized that he was in for an unwelcome visit with his brother. What would he ride him for this time? Would he attack Victor for taking the pain meds he abused to block out his physical and emotional pain? Maybe he wanted to talk about the drinking? Maybe he was just here for the hell of it? He readied himself to get up to answer the door.

Harry wasted no time. He knocked before Victor adjusted to sitting upright. As Victor heaved himself off the couch with a mighty effort, Harry burst through the unlocked door. Briefly annoyed, Victor the look on Harry's face.

"What happened?" he asked solemnly.

"Is Emma here?" Harry solicited, not answering his question. But, in a way, this *was* an answer to his question because he would have no reason to ask such a thing if Emma was where she was supposed to be.

"No. She hasn't been here since her visit."

What a visit it had been. Victor and his daughter said their farewells at the train station. Neither of them acknowledged the disaster that was Emma's foray home. They weren't in contact. Victor thought he could happily pretend that she had never returned home. Though the memories of Emma's visit were horrible for him, Harry's troubled expression made him think this could change.

"Are you sure? You haven't seen her around town or anything?"

"No, she's definitely not around," Victor said slowly. "Why?"

"If you had a goddamn phone, you'd already know why!" Harry snapped. "Emma's missing. Her roommate called this afternoon and told me that she hasn't come home and she can't get ahold of her. She's worried about her, and I am, too. You should have been the one that got the call, but you won't get off your ass long enough to pay your phone bill."

"Emma's missing?" Victor mumbled, trying to process this horrifying news.

"Yes! Try to keep up, Vic. We need to figure out what to do about this."

"*'We'* don't have to do anything," Victor said. "I'm going to the city to find her. What you can do to help is bring me to the train station and let me borrow your phone."

"I'm not your errand boy, and I don't want to take you to the train station because you're too drunk to get there on your own."

"I'm not drunk!"

"You could have fooled me. You smell like booze, and this place is a dump. Maybe there was a reason why Emma didn't want to stay here any longer."

This crossed a line for Victor. He stepped forward, jabbing a finger into his brother's chest. "Don't talk about my daughter and me like that!" he said in a raised voice. "You don't get to barge in here and pretend that you have any idea what our relationship is like!"

"I didn't even mention your relationship!" Harry retaliated. "It seems like you're getting pretty defensive. Maybe you *do* know how toxic you are."

Victor was opening his mouth to reply, but Dakota pushed between the two of them and whined. Dakota's interruption grounded Victor, and he realized that he needed to change his focus.

"Let's pick this up later," he said in a cooler tone. "Can I use your cell or not? I want to call Emma's roommate and talk to her myself."

Harry withdrew the phone from his pocket and handed it to Victor.

"She's the last person who called, so her number is right there at the top," he said.

Victor tapped the recent calls icon, found the number, and dialed.

It rang for a while, but just before heading to voicemail, someone answered.

"Hi, Harry! Have you heard anything?"

"This is Victor Nash. I'm Emma's dad."

"Oh, hey!" Maddie sounded surprised. "Have you heard from Emma?"

"Listen, tell me about Emma."

"Is she with you?" Maddie asked again. Her tone was hopeful.

"No, I'm afraid not. I don't know where she could be. Do you?"

"No, I hoped that she was with you. She didn't come home after work, and she has my car. I have no idea where she went. She doesn't answer my calls."

Victor considered for a moment, then came to a decision.

"I'm going to come to the city to look for her," he said. "Would you be willing to meet me once I get there?"

"Sure, yeah, that would be fine. I want to get her back, too."

"Thanks, Maddie. We'll be in touch."

"Okay."

"Bye."

Victor hung up and started to return the cell phone to Harry, who looked at him incredulously. Harry indicated that Victor should keep the phone.

"Victor, this is a job for the police. The only reason I came here was to tell you what was going on and make sure she wasn't here."

"I don't care," Victor said stubbornly. "I'm going, Harry."

Harry realized there was nothing he could do to prevent Victor from leaving. "How long will it take you to pack?" he asked flatly.

"Five, ten minutes tops."

"I'll take you to the train station. Hurry."

"Thank you. Will you take care of Dakota while I'm gone?"

"I don't really want a dead dog on my hands, so I guess I have no choice," Harry said begrudgingly.

Victor clapped Harry on the back. "Thank you."

"It's fine. Just try to figure out what's happening with Emma."

Victor left Harry behind in the living room so he could dig a suitcase out of the closet in his bedroom. His mind cleared, and his focus sharpened. Emma might be missing now, but he would find her. He needed to search. Emma was his daughter, despite their differences. He needed to find his baby girl.

CHAPTER TEN

The train ride to Minneapolis marked the longest interval that Victor had remained sober in a year. He packed whiskey in his suitcase, as well as his less-than-half-full painkiller bottle, but he couldn't drink in his coach seat, and he needed to be alert on this journey to find Emma. Getting drunk or high was unacceptable on this trip. His mission required sobriety until he found his daughter. Intoxication lessened his chances of doing so.

Victor approached the ticket counter and secured the soonest train to the city without incident. It would be arriving relatively soon, and given the small size of their train station, there was no trouble locating the correct platform. He sat on a bench to wait the few minutes and surveyed the other would-be passengers around him, catching sight of a young woman with raven dark black hair and jade eyes. For a fleeting moment, he saw Lily as she'd had been in their youth, walking past him, not looking his way, and felt a wave of grief flood over him. First Lily, and now Emma. What would become of his family? Shaking himself away from the thought, he focused instead on his daughter. Had she simply run off, or was she in grave danger?

Victor tried to sleep during the train ride, but he didn't get a wink. That didn't surprise him in the least: how was he supposed to relax after the news that his daughter went missing? Any parent who *could* sleep soundly would be the odd one out. Victor worried about her last trip home being the reason for her disappearance. Emma wasn't in good shape—that much was clear. In fact, she reminded him a lot of himself, which led to his telling her not to end up a loser like her dad. Seeing so much of himself in her frightened him, though not as much as her disappearance. Victor's fright exceeded any scare he had ever experienced. When he lost Lily, his awareness of it was immediate. He knew she didn't survive. Lily very clearly hadn't been okay. Emma... well, Victor hoped that Emma still had a chance to be alive and well and that he had a chance to become a better parent.

After what felt like the longest journey of Victor's life, he arrived at the Minneapolis depot. Although it was evening, Victor wasn't tired. He craved whiskey, but he wasn't sleepy. Thoroughly engaged in finding Emma, his senses remained sharpened.

After dropping his brother at the Grand Forks train station, Harry, at Victor's request, called Maddie and arranged for her to meet the train. As he disembarked, Victor realized he had no idea what Maddie looked like. The same was true on her end. Could two people who had never met pick each other out of a crowd?

As it turned out, they could. Victor spotted a young woman who appeared to be about Emma's age, standing a little apart from the scattered group of other passengers, family members, and friends. The young woman smoked a cigarette, and she looked a little haggard. Strands of light brown hair hung from her loose bun. When their eyes met, Victor noticed smeared mascara, indicating that she had slept without makeup removal or had been crying. The young woman took a drag of her cigarette and blew the smoke out the side of her mouth as Victor approached her. She straightened slowly and gazed at him warily.

"Hi there," Victor said in what he hoped was a friendly voice. He felt as nervous as this tired young woman appeared to be. He asked uncertainly, "Are you Maddie?"

"Yeah," Maddie said, giving him a once-over. Victor felt uncomfortable but said nothing. "Are you Emma's dad? I guess that's a dumb question. Of course, you're him."

"I'm Victor," Victor said, holding out his hand. He almost didn't expect Maddie to take it, but she did. Her firm grip surprised him as he expressed his appreciation. "Thanks for coming out to see me."

"No worries," Maddie said as she dropped her cigarette and ground it into the pavement with her heel. "I'm glad you made it so quickly. Emma has my car, but we can share the cost of an Uber."

"Sounds good to me."

Maddie eyed Victor's suitcase, taking in information that Victor couldn't pinpoint.

"You packed a lot," she noted.

"It's mostly empty." He grabbed a few T-shirts, two pairs of jeans, socks, and underwear, and all the painkillers and whiskey he could locate. The large suitcase required no effort to lift.

"Are you planning to stay awhile?" Maddie inquired.

"Not if you don't want me to. I can stay at a hotel," Victor replied quickly. He understood the necessity for young women to be wary of strange old men. Maddie appeared to realize Victor's confusion backtracked.

"Not that you can't stay. I just thought that if you packed for a long time, then... then..." her voice broke slightly. "Then you don't think we're going to find Emma very quickly."

Victor realized that she must be looking to him for confirmation that Emma was safe and sound somewhere and that locating her wouldn't take long. Her transparent, almost childlike expression made him want to reassure her, but honesty was best. Maddie was not a child and deserved an honest answer.

"I don't know," he said after a short pause. "Maybe we will, and maybe we won't. I just wanted to be prepared for either scenario."

Maddie nodded, seemingly satisfied with this answer.

"Okay," she replied decisively, withdrawing a cell phone from her pocket. "I'm going to call Uber. Do you want me to use my credit card, and you can give me cash?"

"Sure," Victor said, unfamiliar with how Uber worked. Minneapolis represented urban territory that confused this rural man. "Sounds fine to me. Are we going straight to the police station?"

"I don't think that's a good idea," Maddie sighed. "I spoke with them earlier, and they all but told me Emma was probably out joyriding and sucking…" she caught herself. "And getting high. They all but told me there would be hell to pay if I didn't wait a few days before bothering them again over something that was probably nothing. But they know my car is missing."

Victor considered this for a moment, thinking to argue and insist that they go to the police station anyway, but he held his tongue, knowing he wouldn't be able to convince the police if a scared young woman like her roommate couldn't otherwise. Anyway, if she truly was out getting high, maybe it was better that the police didn't find her first. "I guess we can look on our own for now," he said.

The Uber vehicle arrived at the train station about ten minutes later. The older-model silver sedan seemed more familiar than a yellow taxi. Maddie waved at the driver and motioned for Victor to come with her.

"You take the front seat," she said, sliding into the back. "I don't need as much legroom."

Victor threw his suitcase into the trunk and climbed into the front passenger seat, wishing that he didn't have to make conversation with another complete stranger. Maybe that was the real reason Maddie chose to sit in the back—so she could be silent.

Smart.

The driver was a Pakistani man who spoke little English, so the trio rode in silence. Victor watched the city pass by through a half-open window. The air blowing through it cooled on his face. He wondered what it felt like wherever Emma was. Was there fresh air? Was she driving Maddie's car? Did she run away with somebody? Would she elope?

"Does Emma have a boyfriend?" he asked, turning his head to look over his shoulder at Maddie. She jumped when he spoke, having been in somewhat of a trance.

"Not that I know of," she replied slowly. "I mean, we spend a lot of time around guys, but I don't think she's dating any of them."

Not exactly comforting news, but romance didn't appear to factor into her disappearance. Although, now that he thought about it, elopement represented the least of all evils. The other reasons she could be missing were a lot scarier.

A quarter-hour passed, and the sedan pulled up to an apartment complex and stopped. Victor slid out of the front seat with Maddie following. Removing his suitcase from the trunk, he slapped it, and the driver took off. The car's tail lights strewed a glowing train cutting through the dark.

Maddie muttered to herself as she fiddled with her phone. She secured it in her back pocket and returned her attention to Victor. "Alright, let's get inside. Follow me."

The interior of the apartment reminded Victor of his home, though tidier. The dim light revealed a sparsely furnished room. Victor thought the apartment looked like it belonged to college students. He looked for textbooks, but he didn't see any.

"So, this is where Emma and I live," Maddie announced unnecessarily. "Emma's room is over here and down the hall. You can sleep in there, I guess, unless you want the couch?"

Victor didn't reply, too distracted by the prospect of seeing where Emma spent her time. He hesitated before stepping over the threshold, feeling as though he were violating his daughter's privacy by bursting into her room unannounced.

She's not here, Victor reminded himself, walking past the door frame and flicking on the light switch. Better lighting revealed a room that was a lot messier than the living room. Growing up, Emma had always been neat and organized for her age. The unmade bed and the duffle bag from her trip home lay half-unpacked on the floor. Emma *had* bothered to unpack a bag of coke, which Victor saw on her nightstand, mixed in a clutter of garbage and beauty products. He picked it up and shook his head in disbelief. With all his heart, he wanted to *unsee* this bag and this room. He wanted to return to a place and time where a recognizable Emma existed. He didn't know this version of his daughter.

"Everything look okay?" Maddie asked. Victor turned and hurriedly set down the bag of coke. Maddie's eyes followed the movement, but she didn't seem troubled.

"Is she always this… messy?" Victor inquired. He felt silly for asking, as if Emma's housekeeping habits mattered at this point!

"I don't know. I guess so. She keeps the mess in her room, though, so it doesn't, like, affect the rest of the apartment. Anyway, some of this mess was from me looking for clues."

"Right."

There was an awkward silence, and as Victor was about to speak again, Maddie pointed to the bag of coke. "Does that bug you?" She wanted to know.

Victor was surprised by the question. "Of course, it does," he said. "What parent wants their kid to do drugs?"

"I don't know," Maddie said languidly, examining her finger-nails. "I just thought you would be cool with it, given… you know."

"No, I don't know."

Maddie looked up at him again. "You use, don't you? I mean, Emma's told me a *lot* about you. I bet there's more than clothes in that suitcase."

"Tell me again when you last saw Emma?" Victor asked, intentionally changing the subject.

"Yesterday morning, I think," Maddie said, not missing a beat. Apparently, she was more concerned with finding Emma than pursuing a conversation about Victor's alcoholism and painkiller abuse. "She asked if she could borrow my car to go to work that night. I haven't seen her since."

"Is there anyone else we can call to see if they've seen her? What about some of her friends from school?"

"Uh, I don't think she's got any of those left," Maddie said, giving him a look like *he* was the one who said something weird.

"She hasn't made any friends in school?" Victor asked, frowning. Was Emma really that reclusive now? "She didn't have trouble making friends in high school."

"Oh," Maddie said, looking at him with pity. "I forgot. You don't know, do you?"

"I don't know what?"

"Emma dropped out… like six months ago."

This news hit Victor like a physical blow, and he staggered but managed to steady himself before the shock knocked him flat. Emma dropped out of university? Why? What was she doing instead of going to school? Terrified to ask, but knowing that he needed an honest answer, he asked, "Maddie, where is Emma working?"

"We're exotic dancers. Don't bother going to the club and looking for her. She's not there. I already checked. The people that I asked were rude to me. Don't put yourself through that."

"Emma's a *stripper*!?" Victor exclaimed. Just like that, whatever image of the daughter he remembered shattered. He suddenly comprehended the extent of the damage his isolation and self-destruction had inflicted on his innocent child. What the hell happened over the last six months? Her letters were lies. Emma's life represented the polar opposite of all of the things her parents hoped for her. Victor's heart lay in tatters alongside the dirty clothes and old food containers on the floor. Not only had he lost his wife, but it appeared he had lost his daughter, too. When he found her, and he would find her, he knew that he couldn't look at her as the same sweet child he and Lily raised. Would he recognize her?

Worry about all of this later, something within Victor told him. Later when he cooled off and could be rational about Emma's lies and lifestyle. *Right now, I need to focus on finding her. What happens to strippers and drug addicts who disappear?*

"Did Emma owe anyone money?" Victor inquired once he had

his emotions in check. This seemed like a good place to start. Maddie might not know where Emma had gone, but her dealer probably would.

"I don't know," Maddie said, shrugging. "I don't think so. She paid for everything up-front."

"Including the drugs?"

"Yeah, that's what I'm talking about."

"Are you positive?"

"Look, Victor," Maddie said, putting a hand on her hip, "I'm not Emma's babysitter. If I had all the answers, I would have found her already. You could still be at the farm with your whiskey and your pills. I didn't know what to do, which is why I called your brother in the first place."

"I know," Victor said, realizing that Maddie had likely already shared all of the information she knew with him. "I didn't mean to press you. I just want to find Emma."

"I do, too," Maddie sighed. "I do, too."

The two of them stood in contemplative silence for a moment. The air around them felt heavy with Emma's absence and reminded Victor of what the first few months had been like back without Lily. For a while, he brought lilies and placed them in vases around the house in a futile attempt to retain his wife's presence, but her beloved flowers were no substitute. His feelings at the time reminded him that he felt like a weight-bearing wall had been removed from his home, and he only awaited its collapse. That feeling returned to him in Maddie and Emma's apartment. Two important emotional supports were gone from his soul, and he didn't know if he could go on without them. Missing Lily had been hard enough, but without Emma, life ceased to matter.

Don't think like that, came his rational voice again. *What can we do right now to find her?*

Although it was difficult to decide where to begin searching, Victor had a glimmer of an idea. Even though Maddie reported Emma always paid her dealer, he still thought that he would contact her dealer as the most likely person in her life to know her whereabouts.

"Can you be one hundred percent positive that Emma doesn't owe her dealer money?" he inquired.

"Well, no," Maddie replied, "but it wouldn't be like her not to give him the money. She's pretty good with money. Anyway, he's not exactly a drug dealer."

"Do you know him?"

Maddie looked a little uncomfortable. "Yeah, I mean…"

"Do you think you can get me to him?"

"You want me to do *what*?"

"I want to pay your dealer a visit," Victor answered calmly. "If she didn't pay him, he will want to find her to collect. If she is paid up, he won't want to lose a customer. I think contacting the dealer is the place to start."

Maddie considered this. "Yes, I guess I agree with that," she said at last. "It's possible he knows something, and we don't have much else to work on, so I can take you to see him tomorrow."

"I would appreciate that."

"Okay. Listen, I'm going to get some shut-eye."

Victor said good night and stood absolutely still for several long minutes as he closely observed his daughter's bedroom. Sometimes, he paused in her room at the farm and remembered the happy little girl he raised, missing her but knowing she was off to a new chapter in her life. This room felt different, the emptiness indicating something bad had happened to Emma. This bedroom was deserted because something prevented her from returning. He needed to find her before it was too late.

I'm coming, Emma, he promised her silently. He hoped that somehow—perhaps in her heart—she would feel it.

Chapter Eleven

Maddie smoked a cigarette while she drove, Victor in the passenger seat beside her in the car she borrowed for the day from April. She considerately cracked the window and asked if Victor wanted one. He refused; he might like his whiskey and pills, but he had resisted the tobacco bug so far and planned to keep it that way.

Victor felt beat. Sleep had evaded him the previous night with worry about Emma. His thoughts chased themselves around and around with no resolution. During the few broken hours that he slept, his dreams featured the new version of Emma that Maddie and Emma herself had introduced to him. He dreamt of his girl doing lines of coke from a dirty table in a trashy club. He dreamt of her standing up in an academic hall, throwing her books at a professor, declaring, "I'm done with this bullshit!" Worst of all, he dreamt of her standing on a stage, barely clothed, swaying her hips in front of an ocean of faceless men throwing crumpled dollar bills at her. The worst part about any of these dreams—nightmares, really—was that they didn't vanish when he awakened, covered in a cold sweat. These dreams illuminated a reality worse than he had ever imagined for his daughter.

I hope this dealer has some idea where she is, he thought, watching the city flicker by through the window. He cautiously hoped that Emma had willingly remained with her dealer because he didn't know what that would mean in terms of her physical condition. He dreaded seeing her all coked up, but even more, he hated the idea of her being gagged in a backroom. How could he retrieve her if her dealer kidnapped her? He had formulated no plan beyond getting to the place and asking a lot of questions to whoever was in charge.

"Maddie, have you met Emma's dealer?" he asked, suddenly feeling a lot less confident in his ability to potentially take on a drug lord and his minions.

"Yeah," she said, taking a drag of her cigarette and blowing the smoke through her nose. "He's my hookup, too, when I want a fix. I told you so already."

Ignoring her snide remark, he pressed for more information. "What kind of a person is he?"

Maddie gave a short bark of a laugh. "What kind of a question is that?" she asked incredulously.

"I'm just wondering if he's reasonable," Victor said a little reproachfully. He didn't like being made to feel stupid. "I also want to know how likely it is that he took Emma."

"He's pretty chill," Maddie said. "At least as far as I can tell. I haven't spent all that much time around him."

Victor listened and thought.

"Maddie?"

"Yeah?"

"Do you think he had anything to do with Emma's disappearance?"

Maddie bit her lip, not taking her eyes off the road. "You want me to be honest?"

"Yeah."

"No, Victor. I really don't."

Victor let this sink in but found that it didn't deter him from wanting to make this trip any less. Even if Emma wasn't there, it wouldn't hurt to ask anyone in the dealer's lair if they had any idea of her whereabouts. There was also the fact that the police wouldn't be in touch with this person, and he could be valuable in figuring out where Emma was.

Should I be scared?

Maddie said he was "chill," but how much could he trust her judgment? Victor had once felt confident in his ability to take on most physical challenges, but it had been a long time since he had done any actual farm labor, let alone get into a fistfight. He had permitted himself to get out of shape. He wasn't a weakling by any stretch, but he no longer had lean muscle.

To Victor's puzzlement, Maddie piloted them to the city's outskirts. A suburb was the last place Victor expected to end up today. He had pictured this dealer living in the inner city, not in a nice neighborhood of cookie-cutter houses and well-kept lawns. As much as he didn't want to meet a drug dealer today, he had at least expected it to be somewhere seedy—not a yuppie's paradise with its manicured hedges, decorative mailboxes, and sterile color palettes, no doubt governed by a housing authority. It had been a while since he'd really seen much outside the farm and the small, rural town of Hope River. Something about going from the stark contrast of Hope River to the city and now into this obnoxiously ordinary suburb put him on guard.

"He lives *here?*" Victor asked, waiting to spy on a house that looked out of place or run down.

"Yeah, we're almost there." She gave him a sly glance. "Why, were you expecting some dump? Ike has way too much money to live in a dump."

"I suppose," Victor muttered, committing this name to memory.

Maddie snorted, "Relax, man. Emma does coke, not crack. Get your game face on. We're here."

She pulled up to the curb outside a house that looked like every other one on the block. The curtains were drawn in all of the windows. Victor glimpsed a shadow moving around inside.

Maddie sighed and flicked her cigarette butt out of the window. "Let's get this over with."

"I thought you said this guy was 'chill,'" Victor said as the pair got out of the car and walked up the short driveway to the house.

"He is, but that doesn't mean I like hanging out with him," Maddie said indignantly. "He has a revolving door of losers hanging around. That's why I don't think Emma is here. I doubt she owes him money. Probably a waste of time.

Victor maintained silence despite being annoyed by her attitude. Besides, he had more important things on his mind. Maddie rapped her knuckles on the front door, and Victor realized he wasn't prepared to meet the person on the other side. It wasn't so much that he was worried that he wouldn't be able to handle himself around someone shady. No, it had more to do with the fact that he couldn't stand to think of Emma associating with people like this. Meeting the person who distributed her drugs would make it all real. There was no going back from this, but Victor wasn't about to turn away. His emotional health was definitely secondary when it came to finding his daughter.

After a few long moments passed, and just as Maddie lifted her fist to knock again, someone answered the door. He was a surprisingly handsome and fit man with some stubble and slicked-back, flowing blonde hair. There were a few grey hairs sprinkled throughout his beard. He didn't look particularly friendly, but when he spoke, his voice wasn't angry.

"Can I help you?" he inquired coolly.

"Hello," Victor said, his tone as friendly as it could be under the circumstances. "We were hoping that we could talk to you for a few minutes. Can we come in?"

"Do you have a warrant?"

"Well, no, but—"

The door slammed shut in Victor's face before he could finish his sentence. Victor felt anger igniting in his chest and channeled it into forcefully pounding on Ike's door once more. It took much longer for him to open it again, and by the time he did, Victor's fist was sore.

"God, Victor, cool it!" Maddie exclaimed, but Victor ignored her.

"You don't get to shrug us off that easily," Victor said to Ike, visibly agitated. He felt the tension in the air thicken. "We need to talk to you."

"I need you to get off my doorstep," Ike snapped.

"We're not going anywhere."

"Like hell you're not."

Victor would never know why he did what he did next. Was it because he was unwilling to accept separation from Emma? Was it because he was stressed and at the end of his rope? Perhaps if he relaxed and drank or took more pills, the physical and emotional pain of the last twenty-four hours would go away. Whatever the reason, he punched Ike in the face before his brain told him that was a mistake.

Ike stepped backward, both hands flying to his nose. Recovering quickly, he came back at Victor, throwing a punch that connected painfully with Victor's jaw. Victor launched himself at Ike, and soon, the two of them brawled in the home's interior. The front door opened to a sitting area in which there was plenty of space for the two of them to tear each other's heads off, and for a minute, the fight consumed Victor's attention. Then, he became aware that Maddie was screaming at them to stop, and she had finally wedged her way between them. Their bodies stilled.

"Get the *fuck* out of my house!" Ike spat.

"Not before I ask you about..." Victor trailed off, a photograph hanging on the wall over Ike's shoulder, catching his eye. Really, he shouldn't have noticed it at all, but it was actually a photograph taped over another picture in a frame, and featured in that photograph was... "Why the hell do you have a picture of my daughter in your house?" Victor's sharp voice rang out. He knew that Emma must have been in this house, but why did a drug dealer possess a picture of her, let alone hang it on his wall?

"What?" Ike asked, clearly caught entirely off-guard. "What the hell are you talking about?"

"There," Victor said, pushing past Maddie and walking toward the photograph. Ike tensed, anticipating a blow, but all Victor did was look closely at his daughter's picture. She looked beautiful. Her eyes radiated energy, and she hung on Ike's arm like lovers do. "This is my daughter. Emma. She's who I came here to talk to you about."

"Emma's *your* daughter?"

"That's right."

"Aw, shit," Ike said, running a hand through his hair. "You've got to be kidding me."

"I'm not kidding you," Victor said stonily.

"Well, then you and I had better sit down and talk this out man to man." He gestured to the sofa and two armchairs arranged around a coffee table in the center of the room. For a drug dealer's house, the place seemed perfectly ordinary to Victor.

Victor hesitated before accepting his invitation, but after a moment, he decided that this was better than the two of them beating on each other. He took a seat in an armchair, and Ike took the other one. Maddie perched uncertainly on the couch, appearing as the odd one out.

"So, you're Emma's dad?" Ike raised an eyebrow at Victor.

"Yes," Victor replied, "and she's missing. We thought that she might be here."

"Well, she's not. I haven't seen her in a couple of nights."

"You seem to be pretty close to her, with her picture hanging on your wall," Victor said, unwilling to let the topic drop.

"Yeah, we dated for a while," Ike said, shrugging. "Broke up a while ago."

Victor balked. This guy had to be as old as he was—he was nowhere near Emma's age. Once again, his daughter's image was tarnished. Irrationally, a big part of him resented the man sitting in front of him for it.

"Are you the one who got her hooked on drugs?" he asked.

"Nope," Ike said, meeting his stony gaze with one equally cold. "She was well into that scene when we met. Probably picked it up from some of the other dancers down at the club."

Victor hated knowing about Emma's addiction but resisted irrationally blaming Ike. "What do you know about Emma's work?" It was a serious question.

"I know enough, considering I own the place. Ike Phoenix, of the Phoenix Den. I would say it's nice to meet you, but considering the circumstances…"

That information knocked Victor off-kilter. Ike's presence in Emma's life presented more than he was prepared to assimilate. He had imagined her coming to this place occasionally once her supply ran out. He had *not* imagined her dating this middle-aged drug hookup who owned the strip club where she worked. Certainly, unwelcomed news, but Victor knew he couldn't let himself get bogged down by it.

"You work there, don't you?" Ike asked, nodding at Maddie. "I think I've seen you around."

"Yeah, I do," Maddie said with a small smile. "I'm also Emma's roommate, so you've probably seen us together."

"Maybe," Ike allowed. He paused, then turned his attention back to Victor. "So, you said something about Emma going missing. Tell me about it."

"I don't know," Victor responded. "We were hoping that you could tell us."

"What, you think I had something to do with it?" He snorted at the accusation. "You wish it was that easy. Hate to break it to you, but girls like Emma go missing all the time. I have nothing to do with it. We are strictly business; we haven't been together for a long time.'

"Do you know if she owed anyone money?" Victor inquired, unwilling to be discouraged.

"Hell, how would I have any idea? She always paid for her coke one way or another." Ike stood up, folding his arms across his chest. "Now, it's time for you to get out. I'm sick of you questioning me like a cop. Unless you have actual business, we're done here."

Victor stood, deciding that he didn't want to get into another fistfight. Maddie followed suit, but as Victor headed for the door, Ike stopped him.

"Hey! Just a second. I remembered something."

Victor turned, his heart rising, hoping for a lead to locate his daughter.

"A creep bothered her at the club a couple of nights ago," Ike said. "I saw one of my bouncers throwing him out. If you want to find her, head over there and ask around."

"Thanks," Victor said, genuinely grateful for the intel. "I'll do that."

"I hope you find her. She's good for business."

Victor declined to dignify that statement with a response and left the house. Maddie followed close behind. When the door slammed shut behind them, Maddie tore into Victor like she had been waiting to do it the entire time they were there.

"What was that!?" she scorned him. "You got in a fistfight with him? What the *fuck*, Victor?"

"It's fine," Victor grunted. "Neither of us has any lasting damage. We'll be fine."

I'll just take a few of my painkillers once we get back to the apartment, Victor thought. *That should take care of it.*

"It's not fine! I'll have to find a new hookup, and I could lose my job."

"I'm more concerned about finding Emma than about supporting your drug habit," Victor replied uncompromisingly.

Maddie muttered under her breath as she unlocked the car, but didn't pursue the conversation further. Victor slid into the passenger seat while Maddie lit a cigarette, and settled behind the wheel.

"What a disaster," she groused, starting up the car. "We learned nothing."

"We learned that we need to get to The Phoenix Den," Victor disagreed.

Maddie shook her head. "No, we already knew about the creep harassing Emma. I went to the club yesterday to ask questions, but everyone was an asshole. There's no point in going there again."

"Did you talk to the people in charge?" Victor asked as they drove down the street, back into the city.

"I talked to Kyle; he's like the main bouncer here. But he's an ass with no memory, so I don't think talking to him again will help."

"They might have some idea about the incident," Victor disagreed. "Even if they don't…"

Victor's voice trailed off as he calculated their next step. He wasn't willing to let the search go dead so easily. Paying a visit to the club employing his daughter as a stripper, though agonizing, could provide a clue. A father's love required him to pursue any and all leads.

"I'll talk to the people who were on the floor that night," Victor said, half-thinking aloud, half-talking to Maddie.

"Already did that," Maddie said. "They wouldn't talk to me."

"Ike didn't want to talk to me either, but that didn't last," Victor pointed out.

Maddie glanced at him from the corner of her eye but remained silent, taking a long drag on her cigarette. Unsure if her lack of reaction was his victory or if she was just tired of arguing with him, he relished the silence, suddenly feeling exhausted again. The thought of sitting down with a bottle of whiskey sounded pretty damn good to him. He had a lead that he could follow, but maybe afterward, he would give in and soothe his aching soul.

"I'm glad that you're here," Maddie said after a long silence.

Surprised, Victor reacted, "Why do you say that?"

"Emma talks a lot of shit about you, but you're a pretty good dad. Sure, you're a reckless idiot who needs to keep his temper in check, but I wish my old man cared half as much about me as you do Emma."

Victor considered this, watching the streetlights pass the car one by one. It had been a long time since anyone called him a good dad, and a lot longer since he had felt like one. Maybe once this was over, could Emma see him in the same light as Maddie? All he wanted was the return of his daughter, not just physically but spiritually. Victor desperately longed to recapture the little girl he raised. God willing, it wasn't too late to rescue her.

CHAPTER TWELVE

Victor and Maddie walked into the Phoenix Den at four o'clock. Victor wanted to go earlier in the afternoon, but Maddie insisted that it was wiser to wait a little longer. The manager, Randy Love, might not be there earlier, and the evening bouncers usually began their shifts in the late afternoon. This frustrated Victor, but he knew that she was right. He rejected the idea that there was nothing he could do to shorten the time until he found his daughter. But Maddie insisted this would give them a chance to eat and maybe ice his jaw.

After waiting in the apartment as the hours crawled by, Victor and his sidekick finally stood outside the Phoenix Den. Victor tried to imagine his daughter working here. From the outside, it appeared to resemble most strip clubs he had seen. A flashing neon sign proclaimed the establishment's name above the entry. Other signs advertised: "Topless Girls" and "Girls, Girls, Girls." The establishment called itself a "Gentleman's Club." Although this wasn't his first visit to a strip club, with the realization that his daughter had shed her clothes for a living here, Victor vowed never to enter one again.

"Ready to go in, or do you want to just stare at the sign all day?" Maddie asked, smacking on her gum loudly and staring at him impatiently.

"No, let's get this over with," Victor said, steeling himself.

"Alright."

The two of them walked towards the doors. As they reached for the entrance door handle, Victor noticed that no bouncer appeared to check them before entry.

"Hey, Maddie," he said, pausing. "Shouldn't there be a bouncer out here?"

"Yeah, there should," Maddie said, "but we're usually short-staffed when this shift starts. The girls want security in the back after what happened with Emma. It'll die down, though. We get creeps in here every now and again, and the scare never lasts for long."

"Maybe it should," Victor said, opening the door. "Maybe if there was more security around here, Emma wouldn't have disappeared."

Maddie didn't argue. "Yeah," she said. "Yeah, maybe."

The Phoenix Den's interior didn't come across nearly as seedy as Victor had imagined. Strangely, that small detail permitted him to feel better about Emma spending her time here. Deep red leather and velvet glowed under the dim overhead lighting. Circular wood tables spread throughout the roomy space, with a few close to the prominent stage. On the stage, a young woman gyrated around a pole as a loose collection of patrons watched her as though hypnotized. Victor recalled the old adage about sex workers and strippers "being somebody's daughter" all his life, but now it held an all too real meaning for him. As such, he couldn't bring himself to watch her.

"Okay, so Randy's office is right back there, through that door," Maddie said, pointing. "You can go over there and knock. He might be in, and Victor," she put on a tone of warning. "Randy used to be a bull rider before he started managing here, and his dad's a cop, so don't try fucking with him like you did Ike. If we ever want the police to help, let's not make it worse."

"He was a bull rider?" Come with me so it doesn't look weird," Victor said, not liking the thought of himself, a lone male, trying to get into the manager's office. Maddie's presence validated his presence.

"OK, I guess," Maddie agreed. She stayed by his side as they wove through the tables, drawing the gaze of a young woman balancing a platter of shots and a bouncer standing in the corner, arms folded over his brawny chest. Victor kept his face passive as he stopped before the door and knocked lightly. At the moment, the music wasn't ear-splittingly loud in this club. He was sure that if anyone was inside, they heard.

Victor and Maddie waited.

And waited.

Victor knocked again, a little louder this time. Still, no response.

"He must not be in," Maddie said, her voice a little raised to be clearly heard over the music. "We should just come back later."

"No," Victor said resolutely. "We're staying. I want to be here as soon as he gets here."

"So, what, you want to watch some girls strip while you wait?" She sounded irritated.

Victor understood that waiting was difficult but necessary as they searched for his daughter. "I'll take a seat at the bar and pay attention to my drink," Victor said, unwilling to argue.

"Fine," Maddie said, "but I have a shift late tonight. I'll need to head home to get ready before too long."

"You can always leave," Victor pointed out.

Maddie looked insulted. "She's my friend, Victor," she said. "I care about what happens to her, too."

Consequently, they ended up sitting together at the bar and ordered a couple of beers from the disinterested bartender. A girl listlessly pole-danced on the side of the bar behind the barkeeper. Victor ignored the performance and talked to Maddie instead.

"So, you work *here*?" Victor asked.

Maddie gave him a cross look, but let his accusing tone go unaddressed. "Yeah. The money's good. The crowd could be better sometimes, but it's hard to complain." She took a long drink from her beer bottle.

"Do you ever think about going to back school or anything?"

"I never went to college, but not really. I'd like to think I'll find something else to do someday, but I don't really have a lot of regrets about my choices. I don't exactly have the luxury of loving parents to help me out or anything."

Victor let that information sink in, considering that perhaps he'd been rude asking. "I didn't mean anything by it," he said sheepishly. "It's not like I have any room to judge anybody."

Maddie laughed. "It's fine. Emma told me what you used to be like… what she used to be like. You know that Emma had been talking a lot about 'getting back to herself' lately. So, you must have done something right even if you're not in the best shape these days." Maddie sighed heavily, but continued, "My father wasn't around, you know? So, at least to me, it's impressive how much you love your daughter."

Victor learned that Maddie had plenty to say despite her age and profession. They spoke about her childhood, living with a single mother, constantly having new men in and out of the house, and how it always felt like she was destined to be a dancer, just like her mother. She repeatedly claimed that she didn't mind it, but Victor could sense a certain kind of sadness beneath the surface.

"I'm just glad I'm a little pretty," she added with finality. "Wouldn't get far if I didn't have that!"

"I don't think that's true at all," Victor said, taking another swig of his beer.

Maddie scoffed. "I was never that great at school. Shit, I couldn't even convince a policewoman that another woman was in trouble…"

Victor's face visibly scrunched in anger at the thought of the police ignoring Maddie. "You're smart and capable, Maddie. You're doing a great job, and I couldn't hope for a better person to have Emma's back while I was…" his voice trailed off. She put her hand on his arm for just a brief moment without any further words and then excused herself for a cigarette break.

The conversation became lighter and sparser as they waited. Although she left for another cigarette occasionally, Victor remained at the bar, nursing his beer and keeping an eye out for anybody who could be Randy.

They waited until just past eight o'clock for Randy to show up. Victor had graduated to whiskey and was taking another sip when Maddie's eyes darted over his shoulder towards the door, her eyebrows shooting up into her bangs.

"Oh, hey!" she exclaimed. "Victor, he's here!"

Victor began twisting in his seat, but Maddie grabbed his shoulder.

"No, wait until he gets into his office. Maybe he won't care if you approach him if he has time to settle at his desk before you interrupt him to ask questions." Continuing to wait even longer to interview someone who might know something about Emma's disappearance sounded like torture, but Victor knew she was right. Jumping up and catching Randy before he arrived at his office wasn't the right way to go about doing this.

"Barkeep!" Victor summoned.

The bartender dutifully put down the rag he was using to wipe down the counter and walked over.

"Yes, sir?"

"Give me a double whiskey neat."

The bartender obliged, filling a fresh glass and clearing away the old one.

"Thanks." Victor turned back to Maddie. "Once that drink's gone, we're going back to that office."

Maddie sensed she had little choice, rolled her eyes, and nodded. "You've got it, boss man," she said.

Maddie's anxious demeanor didn't invite further conversation. Victor realized that Emma's disappearance had taken a toll on her too. She had chauffeured him around the city, acting as his tour guide, and introduced him to powerful people at the risk of her job. All he did was be impatient in return. Still, could anyone blame him? Finding Emma wasn't something that could wait or be done on someone else's schedule. Each second she was gone was another second she spent in potential peril. Victor couldn't bear the thought.

"Let's do this," he said, finishing his whiskey in one gulp. He expected Maddie to tell him that they hadn't been waiting long enough, but she didn't.

"Fine."

They crossed the room and found themselves standing outside the same door again. This time, they knew that someone was on the other side. When Victor knocked on the door, somebody *did* answer this time, and he didn't look pleased about the intrusion. Victor tried to imagine the responsibilities of a strip club manager, but he thought it was best to get straight to the point.

"Hello," he said, trying to sound friendly. "I'm a friend of Maddie's, and I'm Emma's father. Could I ask you a few questions?"

"Maddie and Emma, who?" Randy inquired. He was a big man, almost big enough to be a bouncer. His umber skin tone enhanced the broad head with hair shaved close to the skull. His expression and tone radiated hostility.

"Emma Nash," Victor said, only half-answering the question. After all, Emma was the person he wanted to talk about, not Maddie. "She went missing, and this was the last place anyone saw her."

"Yeah, I know," Randy said. "It's a shame because she's a good earner. We miss her on the floor." He turned his gaze to Maddie and gave her a quick once-over. "Do you work here? Because if you don't, I can offer you a position."

"Thanks, but I *do* work here," Maddie said flatly.

"I thought so," Randy said, unfazed. He shrugged. "You have one of those faces that just about any girl could have. Emma was unique. That's why people liked her."

Although Victor agreed that Emma was special, he was paradoxically offended to hear his daughter described like merchandise.

"I heard about an incident that happened a few nights ago," Victor pressed. "Someone was kicked out of the club because of something he did to Emma."

"Right," Randy confirmed. "She was giving a lap dance but the guy was too feely. It happens sometimes. That's just part of the job. Anything else?" He was clearly ready for the conversation to end, but Victor wasn't prepared to let go yet. If Randy wasn't willing to do much talking, there was always another option.

"Do you know the bouncer who was on duty that night? The one who threw the guy out?" Victor inquired.

"I do," Maddie cut in. "His name's Kyle. He usually works during the later shifts, but not always."

"Well, do you know when his next shift is? I want to talk to him."

"Is there anybody on my staff that you *don't* want to talk to?" Randy asked rather beratingly.

"This has to do with my daughter's disappearance," Victor said stonily. "It's important."

"Well, Kyle's already here," Randy said, pointing to a bouncer standing with his arms folded near the exit. "But before you go and harass him, why don't you enjoy a few drinks? Watch the girls? You seem like a guy who could use some time to unwind."

"Thanks for helping us out," Victor said, trying not to sound sarcastic.

"Right," Randy said, closing the door in Victor and Maddie's faces.

"Victor, hold on before you go over there and confront Kyle," Maddie said, grabbing his forearm. Victor wanted to shake off her hand, but he forced himself to look down at her instead. "I want to tell you *again* what I've been telling you since before we got here: I already *tried* talking to Kyle. I already tried talking to a bunch of the people here, and none of them know anything. Kyle is an ass. He didn't give me the time of day. He's not going to answer your questions either."

"We'll see about that," Victor said, undeterred. Now, he *did* shake Maddie off, and he walked swiftly across the room towards the exit. Kyle wore sunglasses, but Victor saw the bouncer's gaze shift to him as he drew closer. He tried to slow down in order to look less aggressive, though he realized it was probably not successful.

"Your name Kyle?" Victor halted in front of him, noting the man's enormous muscles and impassive expression.

"Do I know you?"

"No, but you know my daughter," Victor said. "Emma Nash. She works here. The other day, you ejected someone who was getting grabby with her. Do you remember that?"

"Yeah, I remember," Kyle said expressionlessly.

Victor waited for him to say more, but he didn't.

"What did the guy look like?" Victor pressed on after an awkward pause.

"I'm working here, man," Kyle said coldly. "Go and interrogate someone else."

"I'm just asking for a minute of your time," Victor said, unrelenting.

Kyle uncrossed his arms and straightened up. "And I'm telling you to get lost," he fired back.

Victor bristled, straightening up himself. "My daughter is missing. I know that you must be really busy standing here with a stick up your ass, pretending you're in fucking *Road House*, but I'm not going to give up that easy. Now try to use what's left of your steroid-juiced brain to remember what the guy looked like."

Something in Kyle's expression hardened. "Alright, buddy," he growled. "You're out of here!"

Kyle attempted to grab Victor, but Victor swatted his hand away. Considering what followed, this may or may not have been a mistake. Yes, Victor had had a few drinks, but that had been over the course of several hours. His anger overflowed. When Kyle swung at him with force, Victor ducked and led with his fist. He punched Kyle's jaw before Kyle had a chance to react, but it was clear that this bouncer had dealt with his fair share of violent patrons. Shaking off the blow, Kyle gave chase. Victor dodged, and Kyle crashed into a table, knocking it over. Victor observed that Kyle was large, but his bulk slowed him. Victor pondered his next move.

Kyle turned and charged him. Victor aimed for a blow to the midsection, but his fist didn't connect. Kyle grabbed his arm midpunch, twisted the limb backward, and pinned it against Victor's back. He spun Victor and shoved him forward into the wall facefirst. Victor's pent-up anger provided adrenaline-fueled strength. He kicked backward into Kyle's kneecap. As the bouncer's grip loosened, Victor tore free and whirled around, fists flying. He connected on a few punches, but other staff members noticed the conflict and descended upon him like flies on rotting meat. In moments, two goons gripped Victor by either arm, and he realized his rampage was over.

When he stopped struggling, he heard Maddie speaking. She stood some distance away with several other girls, all of whom looked shocked. Maddie's expression displayed anger more than shock, and Victor understood why. It must appear to Maddie that he got into an altercation wherever she took him. If he wanted her to keep helping him look for Emma, he needed to control his anger and work with a level head. Why did every man in Emma's life have to be such a hardhead—himself included?

Victor's heart sank when, instead of throwing him out of the establishment, the bouncers holding him in place dragged him to where Randy stood just behind his girls, looking disgruntled.

"You're a real piece of work, you know that?" he spat.

Victor had heard worse, but he didn't say so.

"Your bouncer refused to answer my question. I refuse to leave without some useful information about my daughter. Her life could be at stake."

Randy sighed and massaged his temples with his fingertips. "Jesus Christ, Kyle, just answer the man's fucking question."

"What do you want to know?" Kyle growled. Victor's blow had split his lip. He dabbed at it and examined the blood with the back of his hand, scowling.

"What did the man who disrespected Emma look like?"

"Am I supposed to remember every guy that comes in here?"

"I'm not asking you to remember every guy. I'm asking you to remember one."

Looking as though he wanted to give Victor a few more good punches, Kyle's brow knitted in thought. "He was a dark, greasy kind of man," he said after a moment. "Long, black hair—curly. I don't remember anything about him other than that."

"There," Randy snapped. He pulled his fist back so quickly that Victor didn't have time to react and delivered a solid punch to Victor's nose. "Now you have your answer, asshole. Split."

He nodded at his goons, and they roughly yanked Victor backward toward the club's entrances. Victor didn't resist; he was too busy digesting what he had just been told and absorbing the pain in his nose. Was he happy to have a description of Emma's harasser, or was he devastated that he didn't have more details?

Victor heard the front doors open, and a moment later, his ass collided with the sidewalk. He picked himself up, disoriented, and dusted himself off when Maddie exited the club to join him. She wasted no time chewing his ass for his latest stunt.

"Well, that went well! You're fucking insane, Victor!" she shrilled. "How do you always end up trying to murder the people you say you just want to talk to? I can't keep doing this with you."

"Maddie," Victor replied in a steady voice, completely drained and not ready for another argument. "Now is not the time to confront me. Yell at me later. Right now, I just want to get back to the apartment."

"You're *so* lucky I'm even going to let you come back," Maddie groused, walking down the sidewalk without him. "I'm only letting you stay with me because I care about Emma. You're an asshole."

"Thanks for letting me stay," Victor said genuinely as he caught up to her. Ass or not, he was grateful for a place to stay while he hunted his lost child.

"Whatever."

As they strode away from the Phoenix Den, Victor glanced over his shoulder. This glimpse of Emma's life was a nightmare for him as a father, but he realized he needed to understand this part of her. When he found her, he would see her for who she was and not for who he wanted her to be. The 'All American Girl' stereotype died and was replaced by Emma Nash, his beloved child.

CHAPTER THIRTEEN

Maddie was nowhere to be seen when Victor woke up in the morning, and that pissed him off a little. He needed a way to get around the city and a brainstorming partner, and now he didn't have either. The vague description of the person that had been thrown out of the Phoenix Den the day Emma disappeared was all he had to go on, but it was the first real break in tracking her down.

"Where the hell did Maddie go?" Victor grumbled, pacing restlessly around the living room. Sleep eluded him in Emma's room, and "it" overwhelmed him. "It" being the almost palatable absence of his daughter.

Victor opened his phone and contemplated calling Maddie for the sixth time, but he ultimately stuffed it back in his pocket, feeling fairly confident that number seven wouldn't prove the charm. *Why she wasn't picking up? Oh God, what if Maddie was missing too?* Was he being paranoid? Maybe, but a lot of people in Victor's life had already disappeared in one way or another.

Feeling stir-crazy, Victor went into Emma's room and grabbed his remaining bottle of whiskey. As an afterthought, he shook out a handful of his pills, too—his chronic pain starting to ebb back into the front of his brain, and he wanted it gone.

That's not the only reason you're taking them, Victor's inner voice accused him.

Yeah, well, so what? Victor thought back. *I need something to take the edge off.*

He opened the bottle and was just bringing it to his lips when he heard the front door open and close. Keys clicked loudly as they were thrown on the kitchen countertop, and Victor heard Maddie flop down on the couch with a sigh.

"Maddie?" Victor called, setting down his bottle and walking out of Emma's room to the living room.

"Yeah?"

"Where the hell were you?" he asked, coming up behind the couch. Maddie twisted around to look at him, her expression passive. "I've been waiting here for you all day. I've been calling and calling. Were you in some kind of trouble?"

"What? No. I was returning April's car. She lent it to us because I explained why we needed it, but she was only down to let us have it for one night. I had to bring it back to her this morning."

"Would it have killed you to tell me?"

"Who are you, my dad? Chill, Victor."

Victor opened his mouth to say that, *yes, he was her dad*, but he caught himself. His heart clenched, and he realized that although Maddie wasn't his daughter, she was all that Victor had right now. A part of him recognized Maddie *as* Emma, the same part that refused to believe that Emma was gone. Maddie and Emma were probably very similar people, even though Victor found himself reluctant to accept that the two young women had much in common.

"I'm sorry," he said at last. "I just want to find Emma."

"I get why you would be pissed, but it's actually not a big deal,"

Maddie said.

"Finding Emma isn't a big deal?" Victor solicited, getting ready for an argument, but Maddie wasn't interested in fighting.

"No, of course it is! You know that isn't what I meant."

"Then what *did* you mean?"

"We have to take care of *our* lives, too, Victor," Maddie said adamantly. "We're running ourselves ragged trying to find Emma. What happens if we get to a point where we can't even look for her anymore because we've exhausted ourselves?"

Victor's emotional side didn't agree, but he acknowledged that Maddie had a point. He wanted to search for Emma in a way that made sense. In that vein, he decided that it might be helpful for him to try to understand exactly how Emma appeared prior to her disappearance. If Maddie could answer his questions, it might help lead them to her.

"Maddie? Was Emma acting… strangely before she left?"

"No, why?"

"I'm just trying to make sense of why she left in the first place."

Maddie scrunched up her face in thought, drumming her fingers on the armrest of the couch. "Well, she started talking about getting sober, for one thing," Maddie said after a moment. "She also wanted to start going to church."

This news caught Victor completely off-guard.

"Really?"

"Really."

"She said that?"

"Yeah, she did," Maddie said, shaking her head. "Believe me, I was as confused as you are."

"I'm not… confused," Victor said slowly. "It's more that I'm surprised. I didn't realize that she was interested in…" He trailed off, knowing that however he finished that sentence might end up being offensive to Maddie. "Bettering herself" wasn't quite the politest wording in this situation.

"Yeah, I didn't know you guys were religious," Maddie said, not catching Victor's drift.

Victor considered the fact that his daughter intended to get clean and reconnect with her faith. Maybe the old Emma wasn't completely gone after all.

"Did she say why she wanted to do those things?" he asked.

Maddie didn't meet Victor's eyes when she answered, "She said that it was what her mom would have wanted, and…"

"And what?"

"And that she didn't want to end up like you."

Now, *that* hit Victor's soul. It wasn't as though he didn't understand why Emma would say that, but he hated the thought that his child saw him that way. If he were stronger, this could present an opportunity to change, but instead, a wave of depression crashed over him. He already knew that he wouldn't do the right thing. Not today. Without a word to Maddie, Victor returned to Emma's bedroom and clutched the whiskey bottle.

Well, so what if I need to numb reality and numb the pain in my body? I'm not defensive. Old habits die hard, and I can't resist. I've been drinking myself into a stupor ever since my wife died. I can't just quit. It's not like I'm drinking instead of looking for Emma. We have no leads.

Victor wandered back into the living room and turned on the TV to watch the local news, holding his whiskey and waiting for the painkillers to kick in. Maddie had evidently gone into her own room, so he only shared the couch with his whiskey. The news brought nothing of interest about Emma, or really anything, and reaching the bottom of the bottle, he still didn't feel numb. He knew it was his last bottle, but he dug through his luggage regardless in hopes that he had forgotten some secret stash of alcohol. Finding a few crumpled bills in his wallet, he decided to find a liquor store. In a city like Minneapolis, there should be one within walking distance.

Stumbling out the door, Victor blinked as the sunlight burned into his eyes. He felt irritated by the fact that it was so bright outside. His world grew increasingly dark, but the rotations of the earth and moon went on without his consent. It was more than clear by now that the entire world—if not the universe itself—was against him. Stumbling away from the apartment, his surroundings blurred, and his mind raced with his helplessness. By the time he found a drab liquor store, he was more than ready to drink the nightmare of his life away. He wasn't so far gone that he didn't realize that he needed to act at least somewhat sober for the clerk to sell him his bottle of Jack Daniels.

"Is that all for you, sir?" the cashier asked dully. She was a middle-aged woman with a nose ring. Victor tried not to stare.

"What? Yeah, that's it."

"Fourteen even."

Victor dug his wallet out of his back pocket and fumbled with the bills, taking slightly too long to withdraw a twenty. The cashier accepted his money without comment. She opened the cash register and withdrew a five and a one, sliding them over the counter to Victor.

"Six dollars is your change," she said. For a moment, Victor thought indignantly that she had overcharged him, but he eventually remembered that fourteen plus six equaled twenty and pocketed the change. The cashier put the bottle of Jack in a paper bag and handed it to Victor.

"Thanks," he grunted. He nodded at her and left the store.

Victor's original plan to walk back to Maddie's apartment and enjoy his whiskey in peace fell apart when he realized he had gotten himself lost in his stupor and self-loathing. He had no idea of how to get back, and between the drink and the painkillers, he wasn't exactly sober. Muttering under his breath, he walked down the sidewalk aimlessly for a minute, coming across a large painting of a rose that looked worse for wear over the years. A mural of sorts, it must have once been a beautiful piece of art, but now it peeled and had crude graffiti tags from less capable artists all along its bottom half. The rose brought to mind Lily's rose tattoo on the back of her neck that held the date "2/19" written with it—their anniversary date. Feeling a rush of emotion, he wanted to drown out the image of Lily's porcelain skin, their wedding, the love he had shared with her before they even knew each other. How appropriate that the rose mural should be in such a worn and disrespected state.

Pushing down his helplessness, he found a bench and sat heavily, placing the sack containing his bottle next to him. He watched traffic for a while, not actually taking in any of the visual data, then decided that he might as well start on his whiskey right there. He rationalized that he didn't know when he would find the apartment, and he had no intention of sobering up out here.

• • •

BEHIND THE WHEEL OF HIS TRUCK, Victor drove down the gravel road that began the journey into town from the farm. Raindrops splatted on the windshield; the wipers frantically swished back and forth, back and forth. Stretching ahead were his family fields, the spring wheat tall and a deep green, yet to flower. Even though the day was dark due to the thick thunderheads obscuring the sky, Victor saw another vehicle in the distance, its headlights blazing through the rain. Buckled into the passenger seat belt, Lily spoke loudly enough to be heard, but her words were unintelligible.

Part of him realized that this was his recurring dream, but he couldn't wake up until it played through.

As the vehicle in the distance grew closer, Victor noticed something in the rearview mirror. Startled, he did a double take and realized that someone was sitting in the backseat. It took Victor much longer than it should have for him to recognize Emma. Her hair hung in greasy strands around her pale face. Deep circles underscored flat, lifeless eyes. Clad in filthy clothing, she slumped in her seat. His daughter's eyes met his own in the mirror. Her face hardened into a glare.

"You're such a loser," she accused.

"I'm sorry," Victor said mournfully. "I'm so sorry. I'll get better, I promise. Just please, for the love of God, come home."

Emma looked away, and Victor glanced back out the windshield just in time to see headlights bearing down on him, and then—

• • •

VICTOR AWOKE WITH A START, sitting bolt upright on the bench where he blacked out. He felt like shit. The bottle of whiskey lying on the ground next to him cued him into why he felt horrible. His dream, while in many ways familiar, had been disturbingly different this time. He had never seen a strung-out Emma in the rear seat before, and he hoped that he never would again.

Rubbing his head, Victor searched his pockets for his phone. He called Maddie, intending to ask for directions, but as he dialed her number, an idea emerged from his alcohol-sodden brain. He wasn't sure where it came from, but he was in no way in a position to turn down a hunch.

Fortunately, Maddie answered her phone and sounded genuinely concerned when she greeted him.

"Victor! Where are you?"

"I'm not sure," he admitted. "I was hoping that you could help me out with that. But more importantly, what church was Emma going to start attending?"

"Um… let me think." There was a long pause. Victor didn't expect her to know, but when Maddie spoke again, she sounded reasonably confident. "I think she would have gone to the one on Purdue and West Line. Do you need me to find you and get you there?"

"No, that's okay," Victor said. "I'll find my own way there."

"You sure?"

"I'm sure."

"Alright. Call me if you get more lost."

"Will do."

When Victor hung up, he felt a little lighter. He could ask directions from someone walking down the street or catch a bus to get closer to the church. Finding his way there didn't feel like an obstacle. He had no idea why he thought going to a church that Emma may or may not have ever visited was a step in the right direction, but he was going to trust his gut on this one. As he got up off the bench and stretched, he decided that even if he was a loser, he was going to be a better dad. He and Emma could go to church together once he found her. And he would find her. Because now, through some sort of divine intervention, he had a lead.

CHAPTER FOURTEEN

Victor had tried to approach several people as he walked toward nowhere in particular, but between his disheveled state and slurred words, the cleaner and more upstanding citizens mostly avoided him or told him "sorry" without having even listened. Finally, asking a drunk slumped on a bench for directions to Our Lady of Perpetual Grace, Victor learned that he wasn't far from the church where Emma most likely had attended Mass a little over a week ago. The bench where he found his drunken brethren also served as a bus stop for a bus line that would bring him near the church's front doors. Victor would not have described himself as a lucky man, but someone upstairs seemed to be looking down and smiling at him for once. At least, that's what he told himself.

He boarded the nearly-empty bus, sitting alone near the middle to avoid the bus driver smelling the alcohol on his breath. Those few minutes felt like a lifetime as he waited for the stop nearest the church, but he kept his hopes high as the bus stopped a few more times, taking on only a few scraggly passengers, all of which remained silent and to themselves, almost ghosts to Victor, whose resolve to find Emma after his bout of self-pity and the nightmare of his recurring dream started to fade behind him. Finally, he stumbled down the steps at the stop nearest the church.

Victor paused on the sidewalk, gazing at the impressive building before him. Built as a giant A-frame, magnificent stained-glass windows on either end permitted sunlight to enter. Compared to St. Mary's, his home church, it was enormous, which made sense because there were a lot more Catholics in the city than in Hope River.

After gazing at the church's exterior for several minutes, Victor entered through the heavy wooden doors. The narthex was deserted, but, gazing down the center aisle, he noticed a priest lighting candles on an ornate altar of dark, polished wood. Victor sat in a pew near the back and gazed at his clasped hands. He felt like a kid coming to his parents to admit a childish transgression. Although he knew that everyone sins, every day, he felt positive his sins surpassed God's tolerance. Could his sins be forgiven because he was searching for Emma? God surely realized that Emma was another lost soul. Did one soul helping another soul cancel sins? Victor doubted it.

"Hello, my son."

Victor looked up, startled, and realized the priest had walked down the aisle to stand beside him. The priest smiled when he saw Victor's expression and held up his hands in a gesture of peace. Victor took in the priest's rugged yet clean face, strong jawline, and the bits of silver streaking through his dark, chestnut hair.

"I didn't mean to frighten you. I'm harmless, I promise. May I sit?" he asked. His gentle voice invited a response. Victor scooted over, and the priest seated himself alongside.

"Are you an out-of-towner?" the priest asked, still smiling.

Victor laughed despite himself. "Do I really look that much out of place?"

"It's more that I don't recognize your face. I know the neighborhood people who come to my Mass. I'm Father Hudson. You don't have to tell me your name if you don't wish, but I'm pleased to meet you."

"I'm Victor," Victor said, deciding to be as open as he could with Father Hudson. He had no reason not to trust him. After all, he was a priest! "Victor Nash."

For a second—no, a fraction of a second, or a mere fraction of a fraction—Victor saw an expression flit across Father Hudson's face that didn't suit his demeanor. The priest's malevolent face registered surprise, but the expression was there and gone so quickly that Victor soon forgot that it happened.

"It's a treat to meet you, Victor," Father Hudson said warmly. "What brings you to this particular city?"

"Well, Father… it's a long story," Victor said, looking away from Father Hudson's wrinkled face. Victor's hands tremble because he knew he had to dredge up repressed memories of his daughter and her disappearance. He strived to control his emotions and maintain his composure. Father Hudson gestured to the empty church and gave him a wry smile.

"Anything you say is between you, me, and the Holy Spirit. I have time to talk."

Victor sighed and then, without further hesitation, dove into his story, avoiding the priest's eyes in his shame. He told Father Hudson about Lily's death, about how it ruined him, about how Emma appeared to be fine initially but not anymore. He confessed his alcohol and drug abuse. He shared his realization that Emma's response to losing her mother mirrored his own grieving process. Victor shared Emma's life since Lily's death: quitting school, becoming a stripper, and abusing alcohol and drugs. "I think she still has potential to turn her life back around if I can just find her," he declared and continued his confession by relating why he came to the city to search for his daughter, how he's staying with her exotic dancer roommate, and visiting places and people who could lead him back to her.

As Victor's voice silenced, he glanced at a window near the altar that looked out on a small cemetery to the rear of the church. A gravedigger labored alone, marking out a fresh grave. Before he could look away, something caught his attention. A quick chill ran down his spine like a deep-seated and primitive part of himself was on alert.

"Father, who's that?" he asked, pointing all the way out of the distant window.

Father Hudson looked puzzled by the abrupt shift in topic but followed his finger.

"Who? Oh, that's just Mr. Crane. He's been helping me out here for a long time."

"What does he do here? Does he just dig graves?"

"For the most part, yes. He's a simple man but kind. He has a troubled past and finds solace here in the house of the Lord."

"What kind of troubled past?" Victor asked. It was an invasive question, but Victor asked anyway, eyes fixated on the man rhythmically shoveling dirt out of the hole in the ground.

"Well, Edward was abandoned at an orphanage when he was a child. His mother was a prostitute and an addict who couldn't take care of him. He went from orphanage to foster home until the church social worker found him living on the street. After a while, he found refuge here. He's a good man." Father Hudson elaborated, "I relate to his story because I am an orphan, too. Unlike Edward, I was adopted into a Catholic family and lived a very different life."

Victor wasn't as interested in Father Hudson's life story as he was in Edward's. Edward's tragic story, combined with the uneasy feeling he had about the handyman, disturbed him. Did Edward notice Emma during worship? Emma's beauty, inside and out, lit up every room she entered. Most people found it difficult *not* to notice her, although Victor knew he was biased. He believed that, along with her mother, Emma must be the most beautiful woman ever born.

He wondered darkly if this Edward might have thought the same thing but in a very different way.

Edward certainly fit the description that the bouncer had given of the person stalking Emma. It was a vague description and could have fit half the city, but Victor was willing to grasp at straws. He had little choice.

"Father Hudson?"

"Yes, Victor?"

"What else can you tell me about Edward?"

"That's an interesting question," Father Hudson said, frowning slightly. "What do you want to know?"

"Anything and everything you can tell me about him."

Father Hudson shifted a bit in the pew, looking uncomfortable, but Victor ignored that.

"Where does he live? Is there any way you can give me his address or phone number? I need to talk to him when he's finished working."

"I think it would be inappropriate of me to answer these questions," Father Hudson said, his face serious, his wrinkles scrunched together in concern. Giving a brief, friendly smile, he shifted in his seat again to look Victor in the eyes. "I should get back to my pastoral duties, but I want to leave you with something to think about before you go. You remind me of a man I spoke to once in confession several years ago. I cannot divulge exactly what we spoke about, but I can tell you that anger consumed this man. Revenge is not the way to hush the turmoil within you about your wife and daughter. Violence only begets more violence."

Victor had mixed reactions to this. On the one hand, he wanted to tell Father Hudson to go fuck himself—of *course* he was trying to find and destroy the man who had taken Emma away from him. But, on the other hand, he wanted to listen and think. Maybe if he tried chasing Emma's kidnapper more calmly, he would find better luck in his search. He couldn't beat up every person that Maddie introduced him to. Should he take a leaf out of Emma's book and attempt to get his own life on track while he tried to find her? Could he become a better man by the time he reunited with his daughter?

"Thank you, Father," he said at last.

"Of course, Victor. I am called to guide God's children." Father Hudson stood, drawing Victor's attention to the fact that he was fairly fit for an older man. He couldn't see much of the guy underneath the black shirt tucked into his black jeans, but he didn't have the gut that Victor did. "Come back for Mass, Victor. Our parish would welcome you on Sunday."

"I'll make it if I can," Victor said and meant it.

"Go in peace."

"Thank you, Father."

Victor stood as Father Hudson returned to the front of the church before entering a door to the side of the altar and disappearing from sight. Victor turned to go, but his attention was captured once again by Edward Crane digging the grave just visible out the back window. He moved almost mechanically, and once again, Victor's senses alerted. He felt the hair on the back of his neck stand on end.

Is that you, Lily? What is it?

Victor blinked. Although this hadn't happened before, Lily's voice entered his consciousness fully. What was going on that had every one of his senses on alert? Was Lily trying to help him find their daughter from beyond the grave? Was this just an addiction-addled hallucination?

Checking to ascertain he was alone, Victor jogged up the aisle to the window behind the altar for a closer look at the gravedigger. Edward wore jeans and a dirty T-shirt. His forehead was covered in sweat, which rendered his long, curly hair damp and unkempt. Victor's hand, unbidden, rose to his chest. This guy truly fit the description of the man that Kyle, the bouncer at the Phoenix Den, had given him. The resemblance was so uncanny that Victor wondered what he was supposed to do next. Call the cops and tell them to take this monster into custody? No, he couldn't do that. Other than fitting a vague description, there was no definitive evidence implicating Edward in Emma's disappearance. He couldn't act on sheer emotion alone.

"Victor?"

Victor spun around and saw that Father Hudson reappeared from the door he had disappeared into minutes before. The welcoming voice of the priest disappeared, and his expression had hardened. Victor wondered if an attack was imminent.

"Father, I—"

"You need to leave."

"But Father, I need to talk to you about—"

"Now, Victor! I will not allow whatever is happening here to continue. Leave peacefully."

Victor knew it was senseless to argue further, so he obediently walked back down the aisle, glancing over his shoulder once to see if Father Hudson still watched him. The priest stood at the foot of the altar, his expression cross and his arms folded over his chest. Victor instinctively knew that it would be in his best interest not to return. However, if this was his only means of contact with Edward, he had no choice. As he walked down the long center aisle, Victor came up with the beginnings of his next plan of action, however dangerous or misguided it may be. With all his heart as her father, he knew he had to do whatever it took to find Emma, even if he had to break some laws in the process.

CHAPTER FIFTEEN

Victor waited until nightfall and the cloak of darkness to carry out the plan he had settled on only hours before. Without telling Maddie what he was doing or why he had been away for so long, he watched the church from across the street. Having seen no rectory on the grounds, Victor expected the priest to leave for the night eventually. After waiting for what seemed like an eternity, Father Hudson finally finished his priestly duties and shuffled out to the parking lot. The priest entered his car and drove off. Victor hoped that meant the church was entirely empty of occupants.

Victor wasted no time crossing the deserted road and walked towards the church. The building towered above him, still grand and beautiful even in the darkness. After staring at it for several hours in wait, it somehow seemed larger than it had been when he entered it earlier in the day. Victor realized that breaking into a church to investigate was a new low, but having gotten no news from the police, desperate times called for desperate measures. Something about that gravedigger stuck in his brain like a thorn, and he couldn't afford to ignore it since it was his only possible lead. Every instinct required his full attention, even if it meant doing things that he might later regret. If it helped him save his daughter, surely the Lord would forgive him. The law may not see it that way, but there was nothing he could do about that now.

Victor walked around the large church building and looked for the best way to gain entry. He walked the cemetery's fenced perimeter; the grounds were well-kept, and the graves were all tidy. In the darkness, the headstones shined slightly with the few dim lights from the surrounding area. The angelic figures of a few larger statues almost seemed to be watching him, already aware of what he planned on doing, judging him, perhaps even wailing against his transgressions. A headstone not unlike Lily's caught his eye for a moment, but when he scanned it, the words and dates seemed too worn with time to read. Would Lily's go forgotten this way?

Given the grim circumstances, an eerie feeling came over Victor, but there was nothing particularly helpful in this search around the graveyard's perimeter. The front doors appeared to be the weakest point because they had windows to break, allowing him to reach inside and unlock the deadbolt. Unfortunately, gaining access to the building required him to carry out his actions in full view of any passersby on foot or in cars.

I'll just have to move quickly and be careful, Victor thought, deciding he had to take the risk. The parking lot might put enough distance between the church doors and the street so as not to attract unwanted attention. *How to break the glass?* The stained-glass windows would break more easily than safety glass.

I can wrap my shirt around my fist and just punch it.

Would that work? It was worth a shot, anyway. He didn't have other options unless a hardware store was open nearby at this time of night to sell him a crowbar. It wouldn't do to leave now, though.

Crouching in the shadows, Victor waited impatiently for the

street to be deserted before moving forward with his plan. He pulled his shirt off over his head and wrapped it as securely as possible around his closed fist. If someone drove past by and saw him, he couldn't talk himself out of a clear case of breaking and entering. If law enforcement confronted him, it would divert from the search for Emma. He looked around the street once more to make sure he was truly alone.

Victor raised his fist and pulled it back, but he didn't hit the glass. Standing there with his shirt off, the cold night air mixing with his palpable discomfort at breaking into a church, he hesitated. But why was he hesitating? Every second wasted was another second that Emma would be in the custody of Edward Crane.

Compelled by thinking of Emma's peril, Victor leaned into the punch, hitting the glass with his full power. A combination of adrenaline and fear for his child propelled him through the shattered window until he was elbow-deep. Colorful shards, once religious imagery, dug painfully into his skin. He ignored the blood and removed jagged glass remnants before reaching through and fumbling to unlock the door from the inside. For a moment, he thought there might be a more sophisticated lock than a deadbolt, but when he clicked it to the side, the door creaked and opened. He supposed a church wasn't usually a target for crimes, but he would have thought there could be a bit more in the way of security.

Victor forced himself to get inside the church quickly and shut the door. He threw the deadbolt back on and peeked out the shattered window. No pedestrians strolled on the sidewalk. The street remained deserted.

So far, so good.

Victor unwound the shirt from his fist and shook glass fragments out onto the floor before donning it again, blood from his arm looking like a lazy tie-dye pattern. He prepared himself to investigate. When he turned to face the sanctuary doors, his confidence waned. Even with moonlight streaming through the windows, Victor felt uneasy.

It might only get scarier, depending on what I learn, Victor thought bleakly, walking down the center aisle, tapping each pew as he passed and made his way to the altar. Arriving at the altar, the sanctuary lamp provided faint illumination. Had Father Hudson locked the sacristy after he removed his vestments? What was he supposed to do then?

Deciding that it was best to just test the doorknob and get it over with, Victor wrapped his fingers around it. He sighed, turned it, and…

It opened. The damned thing opened.

Victor almost shouted in triumph but remembered that minimal noise was imperative. The less likely he was to draw attention to the fact that someone was in the church when there shouldn't be, the easier it would be for him to get out. He searched for a light switch on the wall, found it, and flicked it to the on position. Recovering from temporary blindness due to the stark change in lighting, he saw that he was standing in one of three rooms opening from where he stood. It looked pretty standard for a sacristy: a safe with the offering collection money, a special safe containing unblessed sacramental bread, and a great many candles, new and used. Victor walked forward and peered into the first of the remaining two rooms, where he discovered the vestry with hanging clerical garments, stoles and chasubles for each of the seasons of the church year. Victor continued to the third room, which held a desk, an overloaded bookcase, and several sacred paintings.

He paused a moment to examine a painting of a winged warrior, muscular and draped in red, flowing fabric. In one hand, he held a sword high into the air; in another, he held a chain leading to the ground, where the warrior's foot stepped atop the head of what appeared to be a winged demon, ugly, red, and in despair. He recognized the painting as St. Michael the Archangel. He tried to remember what happened in the Book of Revelations, but the details were fuzzy at best.

Snapping back to the task at hand, the desk caught Victor's attention. *Bingo.*

The desk's surface was laden with papers, writing instruments, and a computer screen. Victor thought he could detect an informal organization of the documents at first glance. Victor realized this was likely where Father Hudson prepared the homily and the papers held a future sermon. The religious part of him felt as though he was intruding on something sacred. He pushed it to the side, knowing that finding Emma was his priority. Repentance for the sins he committed tonight could come when he was safely out. His priority was searching the desk for anything to do with Edward Crane.

Looking through the four-drawer desk and keyboard tray appeared to be a simple task at first glance. The reality was trickier. Father Hudson maintained an extensive, though unlabeled, filing system. Manila folder after manila folder crowded each drawer. Some folders held newspaper and magazine clippings; others contained documents. Nothing appears to be about staffing or the members of the congregation.

Failing to find anything interesting, Victor finally found what he sought in the keyboard tray. Father Hudson's black leather address book rested next to the keyboard. Opening it to "C," Victor easily found Edward Crane's information and a ripped black and white photograph acting as a place marker. Victor examined it, reassembling the torn pieces, and noted what appeared to be half of a woman's face and body on one piece and the other part of the body with a young African-American boy that he assumed was Crane on the other. The book contained Crane's phone number and address. Victor stood, holding the book in his hands, pondering his next move. Should he go to Edward Crane's address? Should he call him? Should he call the police?

No, he decided. *No. There isn't enough time. I have to act now if I want to be sure that I can save Emma.*

While it was true that he couldn't be one hundred percent positive that Crane was the perpetrator, something in his gut felt very certain that what he found when he got to that house might be more than he could handle. But this wasn't about him. It was about his daughter.

Victor pocketed the little book and left the back room behind, flicking off the light switch as he walked back into the main part of the church. He closed the door behind him, and with it, he felt a distinct sense of finality creep into his heart. This was the beginning of the end of *something.* A final chapter. To what, he wasn't sure, but something was coming, and like St. Michael the Archangel stomping the head of a demon, he wasn't about to shy away from it. He was going to meet Edward Crane with everything he had, extract what he needed from the guy, and then, hopefully, he would see Emma again.

Everything was going to be okay.

It had to be.

• • •

VICTOR FOUND HIMSELF STANDING outside a shack on a street lined with other ramshackle structures that appeared to house twice as many rodents as humans. Many of them appeared to be abandoned or so run down no one could possibly live inside. The night was noticeably darker in this rundown part of the city, as though God hadn't put enough stars up in the sky for the poor souls condemned to live here. He lingered at the entrance of a building with lights in the windows, but the closed blinds made checking for Edward Crane's presence impossible.

I know the address is right, Victor thought, reassuring himself. *I checked it plenty of times on the way over here.*

Fortunately, the church and Crane's house weren't far apart. Victor had plenty of energy to interrogate Crane if...

If Emma isn't in there.

There was a good chance that she would be, and she might be in bad shape. Victor fully acknowledged that, and the walk had been long enough for him to feel mentally and emotionally ready for that to be the case. He didn't know what awaited him beyond this door, but he did know one thing for sure: he wasn't going to leave empty-handed.

Victor steeled himself, marched to the door, and hammered his fist on it. He listened closely for a response or movement of any kind and got nothing. He heard the television, but that didn't mean Crane was actually watching. Victor moved on.

Alright, then. Plan B it is.

Victor pulled his bloodied shirt off, exposing his pale skin to the chill of the night air, and wrapped it around his hand once again. The window shattered in the room where the television lights had flickered through the shade. A man's voice screamed as Victor one-two-three-hoisted himself through the window and landed head-first on the filthy carpet. He gritted his teeth against the pain in his hand. This glass hadn't been nearly as flimsy as the glass at the church. His knuckles ached as if they had hit a brick wall, and he suspected a bone might be broken. Victor put the pain aside and readied himself to take action that could potentially save Emma's life.

"What the *fuck,* man!"

Victor quickly rose from the floor, still shirtless, the blood running from new wounds and old, but his heart and body ready to fight. He peered around the dingy room to locate the voice and saw a man sitting on the couch, the only furniture except an end table and TV stand.

"That was my fucking window!" the man yelled in shock. He was indisputably Edward Crane with his dark complexion, greasy curls, hardened face, and slouchy posture. His face and voice were blank with shock. "Who the hell are you?"

"I'm going to be your worst fucking nightmare if you don't tell me exactly what I want to know!" Victor said heatedly.

Crane's expression changed. Shock melted away like mud off of a waxed car. His eyes registered alertness, but he showed no apparent signs of fear. Rather, he became more relaxed, almost as though he'd invited Victor into the home himself. A chill crept down Victor's spine. Crane reached for the beer on the end table, took a swig, and slowly replaced it on the wooden end table covered in old food, scratches, and sticky liquid rings from neglect.

"You must be one of the dads, or are you one of the *daddies*," Crane said sarcastically, eyes flicking between the TV and Victor as though he was only slightly interested in the home invasion and the stranger in his home.

Victor's self-restraint loosened as he strode over to where Crane lounged so carefree. He overturned the end table with a swipe of his hand, the beer bottle shattering across the floor as the table landed on it. Victor hauled Crane up by his sweat-stained collar. Crane swung, but his arms were thin, and his belly bulged. Victor's neglect of farm work hadn't diminished the muscle he had built up doing physical labor over the years. Deflecting Crane's blow easily, he answered it with one of his own, connecting with Crane's gut.

"Ugh!"

Crane doubled over, but Victor didn't pause. He grabbed Crane's head and slammed his knee into it, sending Crane toppling to the floor. Victor sneered, adrenaline pumping, and dropped to his knees, straddling Crane's prone body. Victor's left fist, positioned to smash his adversary's face, suddenly opened as Crane slashed his fingers and knuckles with a sharp, jagged piece of the broken bottle. Victor cried out in pain, jumped up, staggered back, and looked at his throbbing hand. Blood surged from the wound, so much blood that it was impossible to see the cut's depth. What Victor *did* know was that it hurt like a bitch, and there was no way he was going to be able to punch with this hand for a while.

Victor looked up to note Crane pulling himself to his feet, a large shard of glass still clutched in his hand, which dripped with blood. It was unclear if it was Victor's or his own.

"I thought you were here to ask questions, you prick," Crane hissed. "What, were you afraid that you wouldn't like the answers?"

Victor wanted to run at him, but he hesitated because of that damn glass shard. Crane didn't miss a thing.

"You're not so strong now that you don't have surprise on your side," he sneered.

Victor laughed. "Oh, you're wrong about that, you ugly prick," he said and charged. He pulled back his good fist to make it look like he wanted to hit Crane in the face, but when it came time to deliver the actual blow, he struck Crane's kneecap with his boot. While expecting to parry Victor's fist, Crane clearly hadn't prepared for an attack from below. Already reaching out to stab with the glass shard he held, most of his body was now left vulnerable to attack. He collapsed to the floor again, this time landing on the end table with a nasty *CRUNCH*. The shard of glass flew from his hand and out of reach.

Victor didn't wait for Crane to rise. He grabbed Crane by the collar and beat the shit out of him until Victor was winded. When he was positive that Crane wouldn't get up, he backed off and took a deep, steadying breath, trying to ground himself and take in as much as he could about his surroundings. Deciding that he had to keep his adversary in place while interrogating him, he decided to search for a chair and something to tie Crane to it.

"I mean, if there *is* rope somewhere here, it would be great," Victor muttered, exiting the living room and entering a filthy, outdated kitchen littered with empty beer bottles and cans, food wrappers, and mysterious sticky spots all around the counters. He saw a wooden chair pushed up against a folding table that would work just fine. He noted it and then moved on, walking deeper into the house.

It occurred to Victor as he walked down a short, dark hallway that Emma could be bound and gagged behind any of the two doors it contained. He opened both quickly. The first door concealed a closet full of soiled clothing and boots. The other door revealed a bedroom not much larger than the closet. Victor stepped inside the latter, gagging a little at the smell. The stench emanating from the room wasn't that of rotting meat but of body odor produced by the piles of dirty clothes cluttering the floor. Kidnapper or not, Edward Crane had issues.

Victor checked in the bedroom closet, under the bed, and in the bathroom connected to the bedroom, but he found no sign of Emma or anyone else. Even so, he was not ready to feel discouraged yet. He hadn't thoroughly investigated the hall closet. There might be something in there he could use.

Victor returned to the hallway, grateful to be out of the bedroom stench, and closed the door behind him. He opened the small closet once more, pawing through hanging raincoats and jackets. Piles of shoes and heavy boots, muddy and worn, littered the floor.

There's nothing in this place I can tie that bastard up with, and he could be up at any minute, Victor thought despondently. He was about to close the door and keep looking somewhere else when he did a double take.

Shoes.

Shoe*laces.*

He could use shoelaces to bind Crane to the kitchen chair! Some of them looked plenty strong, and there was enough to double up to make them more difficult to escape. Besides, even if he *did* get out, Victor wasn't going to let him get anywhere. He was in control of this situation, not Crane.

Victor returned to the living room, double-checking that Crane was still unconscious. Finding that to be the case, Victor donned his bloodied shirt once more before he commenced his shoelace harvest. Boot laces were stout and heavy-duty. He would use those to secure Crane and retain the rest for backup. He piled his spoils on the kitchen' folding table and dragged Crane—who was beginning to moan and move around—into the kitchen with him. Victor heaved him onto the chair, bound his hands and ankles, and backed away, examining his handiwork. It looked secure. *You're not going any-where, you slimy fuck.*

His face damp with sweat from the fight and the search, Victor paused to gather his thoughts as he went back into the living room to put back on his shirt. The bloodied hand seemed to be finished bleeding for the time being, but it ached severely. He would have no choice but to ignore it for now, and returning to the kitchen, he looked upon Crane with disgust.

Interrogation commenced. Victor hadn't anticipated the fierce fight with Crane, but he could spend as much time here as needed. As much time as it took to determine Emma's location and condition. He would not leave without that knowledge.

Anger stoked, Victor slapped Crane to rouse him. The bound man, bruises and lumps already forming on his face in a colorful collage, stirred and looked up. Victor felt no remorse.

"Welcome back," he said.

Edward Crane spat at him in response.

"Oh, so it's going to be like that, huh?" Victor said, cracking the knuckles on his good hand one by one with his thumb. "I'm pretty sore, but I think I can go for round two. You look like hell, but maybe you've got your second wind. What do you say? I'm not going to untie you from that chair, though."

"Fine! What are you doing all of this for? What do you want?"

"I want to know where my daughter is and what you did to her."

"I don't know what you're talking about."

"Yes, you do," Victor said, unfazed. "I'm not leaving this shithole until you tell me."

"You're going to be here for a long time, buddy. Better make yourself comfortable."

Victor could tell that threats of another thrashing wouldn't get him as far as he wanted with this man. He might be able to weasel one or two more clues out of him, but if he had done all the horrible things that Victor suspected him of, he knew better than to open up about them so readily. Unfortunately, Victor had nothing to hold over his head to encourage him to talk. Crane didn't have any family or any friends that Victor knew of, but even if he did, wouldn't doing something to them make him just as much of a monster as Crane? He couldn't stoop to that level. No, his method needed to have something to do with Crane directly.

I'm going to have to torture him, aren't I? Dear God, forgive me.

Victor wandered around the kitchen and checked the drawers. He needed pliers, but would Crane own any? He barely had anything in the way of silverware, and most of the drawers were empty with the exception of a couple of dead bugs. He was about to give up when he slid one open that contained tools and odds and ends— things that you might keep in your kitchen if you had nowhere else in your house to put them.

"What are you doing over there?" Crane asked. His tone was casual, but Victor could tell that he was a little uneasy. His back was to Victor, so he could only hear the sound of him sifting through the items in the drawer.

"Just looking for something," Victor replied nonchalantly. "It won't be a problem for you if you don't make it a problem. Oh, here we go!" Victor held up a pair of pliers triumphantly. "We're in business."

He walked back over to where Crane was being forced to sit and clicked the pliers in front of his face, smiling humorlessly at his captive.

"I'm going to ask you again. Where is my daughter?"

"Or then what? You're going to pull my teeth out? You don't have the guts."

"Where is my daughter?"

"Is that all you can say? She must have been pretty stupid if she had you as her dad."

"Fine. We'll do this your way."

Victor grabbed one of Crane's bound hands and crushed it, leaving only one finger sticking out. He could feel Crane struggling to get away, realizing what was going to happen next, but his hands were quite literally tied. Crane's fingernails were long and filthy, and getting the pliers to hold onto one of them required very little effort. Victor inhaled deeply, looked away, and squeezed as hard as he could. Victor pulled backward, resting his injured hand on Crane's shoulder to ensure that his body didn't follow the direction of the fingernail. Crane screamed, and Victor let him. This neighborhood appeared as if screams in the night weren't uncommon or a cause for alarm.

Victor loosened his grip on the pliers, allowing the loose fingernail to fall onto the cracked tile as blood poured from Crane's injured digit. Teeth clenched in a snarl, Crane breathed heavily, clearly trying to control his pain. Folding his arms across his chest, Victor leaned on the table and pretended that he wasn't feeling sick to his stomach. He hoped that he didn't have to do that twice.

"Where is my daughter?" he asked coldly.

Crane's tear-filled eyes met his, full of hatred.

"I don't know who your fucking daughter is," he spat.

"Her name is Emma Nash. And I think you *do* know her, you sniveling piece of shit."

"I don't know anyone named Emma Nash."

Do I really have to pull another one of his nails? Please no.

"Tell me, or I'll pull another one!"

"Which whore are you looking for? I swear to God, I don't know which one Emma was!"

That made Victor feel sick to his stomach, even though he didn't know exactly what to make of it.

"What do you mean?" he asked, furrowing his brow.

Crane looked Victor dead in the eye, his expression stone cold. "What makes you think that your daughter was special?" he solicited. "Show me her picture. Then I'll tell you whether or not I know where she is."

That was all Victor really needed to hear. He could call the cops right now and get this monster thrown behind bars for the rest of his life, but he still wouldn't have Emma. He couldn't give up until he found her. He owed her that as her father, as her last remaining parent. She needed to know that someone in the world still loved her and would do anything to find her and bring her home.

Victor retrieved Harry's phone from his pocket and searched it for a picture of Emma. To his surprise, there were quite a few of them, and near the beginning of the camera reel. Most were pictures of pictures of her. Victor realized that Harry had ensured to have pictures of Emma on hand to show the police or someone who might know where to find her.

Smart.

Victor was grateful. If not for his brother's foresight, he might have been empty-handed. He lamented that he hadn't taken the picture of Emma hanging in Ike Phoenix's house. Second-guessing his actions wasn't useful, though, and only served to distract him, probably because he was terrified of the possible answer to his question. His courage returned; this was for Emma.

Victor found a good picture of her and turned the phone, enabling Crane to see the screen. Crane's eyes flicked over the image, and a slow, sickly smile spread over his face.

"You mean *that* Emma," he said. "Yeah, I know her. She is something else. I asked for her in person just so I could get a taste before I did the whole thing, you know what I mean?"

Victor waited for the pain to engulf him, but a wall of denial held it back.

"Bring me to her now!" he said aggressively.

"I'll lead you to where she is. That's the best I can do."

Victor gave him a curt nod. "Okay," he agreed. "Let's go."

Chapter Sixteen

Victor tied Crane's hands behind his back before they left the house and kept his hand on his shoulder so he wouldn't escape. Crane didn't seem to care anymore, or if he did, he wasn't showing it. Had he met his match in Victor? Or was he plotting something? Whatever the reason for his current docility, Victor appreciated the break. He felt numb, but a tempest brewed despite his feigned composure, waiting for words that would pierce a hole in the protective cover around his emotions. Crane led the way, but to Victor's surprise, he seemed to be retracing his steps from earlier.

From the moment he heard Emma was missing, his paternal instincts engaged and he devoted himself to her pursuit. Unlike the police, *he* was the one who had pieced together the clues that ended with Edward Crane. *He* was the one forcing the battered Crane to show him where Emma was being kept. *He* was the one the one brave enough to face terrible men in pursuit of justice.

As they plodded along, Victor could see they were heading toward the church and turned into its parking lot, a sinking feeling wretched at his gut. Was Crane planning something nefarious and baiting him to common ground? Emotions reeling, Victor inhaled sharply and forced himself to calm. He couldn't break down until he had Emma in his arms again. He tried. It wasn't easy, but he tried.

"Where are you taking me?" Victor growled in Edward Crane's ear.

"We're almost there," snickered Crane, leading him up to the small church cemetery he'd explored earlier that night, which lay on a flat, well-mowed grassy lawn. Victor wondered if Father Hudson kept Crane on staff for that reason.

Victor and Crane walked through rows of graves, each stone different, some garnished with flowers. This was clearly a place that people visited often. Victor imagined that the location comforted those who came to pay their respects. The moon cast eerie shadows over the grass and the large stone statues, the shadows resembling moving human forms. Victor's heartbeat quickened with excitement. He wanted so badly for the shadow to be Emma.

She's okay! Oh, God, thank you, she's okay! Even though there was no sign that this was the case, Victor repeated these words to himself like a mantra.

Crane stopped suddenly, and Victor barely avoided a collision. He released Crane's shoulder to steady himself. Would Crane run? Had he halted at a random grave and just brought Victor here as a rouse to escape?

"We're here," Crane muttered, a smile curling at the sides of his mouth.

"Where is she, you bastard?" Victor shoved the grimy man hard as he took in his surroundings, spotting the storage shed he'd seen through the window before being ejected from the church by Father Hudson. "Is she in there!?"

Victor rushed to the shed, nearly falling over himself, grabbing at the doors and jerking them hard against the padlock that kept it closed. The rattling of the doors led to splintering sounds as he put his full strength into trying to rip them off their hinges. "Emma!" he screamed out. "Emma, are you in there?" Finally, the old wood gave way, the hinges tearing off on the right side and the lack of resistance causing him to fall to his feet as his weight pulled them back in his frantic effort to see inside the precarious structure. But when he scrambled upright and yanked his way into the right side of the doors, he saw nothing inside but a myriad of tools for maintaining the graves. After a moment of disbelief, Victor spun around and charged at Edward Crane once more, tackling him to the ground next to the grave where he'd stopped and waited for Victor to wear himself down.

"Where the fuck is Emma?" he screamed in Crane's face, holding him tight by his stained shirt.

Crane laughed like a screeching bird and pointed to clods of freshly-turned soil at his feet by a headstone. The shovel lay on the ground beside the grave, solidifying Victor's hunch that it was quite fresh. Victor let go of the man and positioned himself to see where Crane was pointing.

"This is Emma Roger's grave?" he said, squinting to read it through the darkness. "Where is my daughter Emma Nash, you stupid piece of shit!?" Victor screamed in Crane's bloodied face

"Don't worry about the headstone," Crane mumbled. "Your whore of a daughter is eight feet down, keeping Mrs. Roger company. Now let me go home."

"I don't understand," Victor said, completely ignoring that last bit. "The headstone says—"

Crane had gotten up on his knees, laughing again. "Don't worry about the fucking headstone! Emma's down there beneath the marble, whether you like it or not, sharing the hole with some bitch in a casket. What? Did you think she was just sitting in a shed behind the church? Tied up for later? Did you think that I would waste that kind of time on a *slut*? I have whores buried underneath fat old fucks all around this cemetery! I—"

The smoldering volcano of feelings in Victor erupted, surging through him, propelling him to lunge toward the shovel, brandishing it in his bloodied hands, and smashing it with as much force as he could muster into Edward Crane's skull. Crane crumpled to the ground, but Victor didn't stop. He smashed down repeatedly, ignoring the blood spatter streaking his face and clothing, ignoring the fact that Crane could no longer be alive with his head beaten nearly flat against the grass. Although an inner voice told him to cease, he mercilessly pummeled Crane's skull. Finally, his heart hammering, the inner tempest calmed enough for him to think again.

He dropped the shovel and fell on his knees, weeping, covered in blood from Crane's head and his own cut hand now bleeding again. The pain didn't matter. The risk of prison wasn't even on his mind. His body a husk, all he could do was recognize that his spirit had died with the hope of finding his daughter alive. His All-American Girl was buried in someone else's plot, and the last time they ever spoke, their fighting, played back in his mind. His life was all but over. He had no way of knowing how long he stayed that way, lost to the numbness, too tired and broken to move. Sirens could be heard sounding out in the distance, but Victor paid them no attention.

Suddenly, his body was being shaken. "Victor! Victor!" the voice rang out.

Looking up, Victor saw Father Hudson's face above him, the wrinkled but chiseled jawline tense with panic. "What have you done, Victor?"

"I found her, Father," Victor said solemnly. "I found Emma. He killed her," Victor cried out, his words garbled in his anguish. "He murdered her. He was a monster. He told me she's buried in this grave…"

"Victor, you have to leave," Father Hudson urged him erratically. "You can't be here when the police show up. I'll tell them what happened…"

Victor didn't respond, his gaze becoming absent once again. The volume of the sirens grew as they neared.

"Victor," Father Hudson yanked Victor upwards deftly, showing strength that seemed out of place for a man of God. The jarring and unexpected jerk of the motion grabbed Victor's attention. "Look me in the eyes." Stunned, Victor locked eyes with the priest. "If what you're saying is true, you need to leave until the police have dug up this grave and found the evidence. Otherwise, you'll…"

"I'm ready for whatever happens next," Victor murmured. "Thank you for worrying, but it's too late."

"You need to leave. Someone must have heard something. The sirens are already starting to get louder. I'll cover for you. I'll tell the police that I didn't see the man that did this…"

With the priest's help, Victor stood on his feet. Although Victor knew he would have to face his crimes, at Father Hudson's urgent requests, he shuffled off into the dark, still covered in blood, numb in both body and mind.

Victor's beaten and bloodied body limped along through the darkness of the graveyard, out into the parking lot, and out onto the sidewalk. He heard the sound of Father Hudson crying out in anguish behind him, blending with the sirens, but the sounds barely registered. He did not look back and instead began sprinting despite the pain as the sirens slowly got louder.

· · ·

THE JOURNEY BACK TO MADDIE'S APARTMENT felt like a thousand miles. Victor was suddenly very tired, as though his body were already anticipating the effects of several days of insomnia. How he was supposed to get through the rest of the night, he had no idea, and the morning would bring with it a host of even bigger problems. He would have to call his brother and tell him what had happened to Emma. He would probably have to turn himself in before too long. Maybe even trying to reach Maddie's apartment was a mistake now, but the priest had insisted so strongly that he would clear things up that Victor felt compelled to take the advice and take the opportunity to gather himself, steel his courage, and decide how to proceed. He wasn't afraid of being arrested, but he felt as though he owed it to his brother and Maddie to at least let them know what had happened first, and he wanted the opportunity for the police to dig up the graves so they could speak on even terms with all the evidence.

Victor tried to trudge on, but as his weariness grew, his vision began to swim, and he knew he had no shot of making it back. He'd considered calling Maddie for assistance but found the phone in his pocket to be dead. He stumbled a bit further, but before he knew it, he found himself lying between a couple of bushes in a park, crying into his bloodied hands and unable to will himself to move another step. He wasn't really sure what time it was when he woke up, but it appeared as though the sun had only been up for a short time. His body ached deeply, and it took him some effort to lift himself up. Now in the light of day, he knew the police were probably out looking for him, but he still wanted the opportunity to at least talk to Maddie first.

Victor was still feeling weak when he finally reached the door of Maddie's apartment and turned the knob, unsure how he'd even made it back without being spotted covered in dirt and blood. The door was unlocked, which meant that Maddie must be home. Could he bring himself to tell Maddie about Emma? Even though he feared saying the words aloud, he didn't think he would be able to keep the truth from her for long, especially not in his current disheveled state. He would have no choice but to tell her everything. Whether that was a wise thing to do to a young lady, Victor didn't know, but there was no way around it now.

She's tough, Victor reasoned with himself as he crossed the threshold and entered the apartment. *She can take it.*

"Maddie?" Victor called, closing the door behind him. No one answered, but she must be home. Maybe she was just in the bathroom or something.

Despite being filthy, Victor dropped onto the couch heavily to wait for her to come out, half out of it.

And waited.

And waited.

Finally, he decided to call her again, this time more loudly.

"Maddie? You home?"

Once again, nothing.

Starting to feel a little uneasy, Victor hoisted himself up with great difficulty and walked deeper into the apartment. If he had been a child, he might have been afraid that something sinister was afoot, but he knew better than anyone that real life was far scarier than monsters hiding under beds. It was entirely possible that Maddie had just stepped out for cigarettes, or maybe she was conked out on her bed after a particularly trying shift. Victor went to her room and cautiously looked inside the ajar door, but even though the lights were on, everything looked and sounded very uninhabited. He pushed the door open the rest of the way to get a full view of her room, prepared to look away at once if she was changing her clothes, but this was in vain; there was no one there, either.

I don't like this.

Victor broadened his search to the bathroom and Emma's room, but both of them were Maddie-free. There weren't very many places for anybody to hide in this apartment, small as it was, and Maddie definitely would have heard him calling her and walking around looking for her. Something was awry.

Victor made his way into the last place Maddie might be: the minuscule kitchen. Unsurprisingly, Maddie wasn't here, either, but there was evidence of her having been not too long ago: a cold TV dinner sat on the counter, the microwave still standing open. Her purse was also there, knocked over with some of its contents strewn over the floor. The Derringer immediately caught Victor's eye and he pocketed it thoughtfully, as if hoping that doing so would tell him what had happened here. Enlightenment eluding him, Victor set it back down again and made to exit the kitchen, but something on the table caught his attention. He hurriedly moved to inspect it and saw that someone had speared a photograph onto the surface, one that had been ripped in half but was now taped together.

At first, Victor didn't think that he recognized the picture, but he realized as he was jimmying the knife out of the table that he actually did recognize one half: it was of Edward Crane as a young boy, the one that Victor had seen in Father Hudson's address book.

Spooked, Victor searched his pockets for the book, positive that he had taken it from the Father's desk, but he came up with nothing. It must have fallen out of his pocket at some point during his journey to Crane's shack, and it had been found by some psycho who had taped it to…

Victor picked up the photograph to look at the unfamiliar half and saw that it was of a young Caucasian boy standing with a woman of the same race, both of them smiling at the camera. One of the woman's hands clasped the white boy's shoulder, and the other rested on Crane's—a detail that Victor had missed when he initially looked at the picture. He flipped the picture over, searching for more information, and found a short message scrawled over the back:

If you want your whore, come to the church alone.

For a moment—one heart-wrenching moment—Victor thought that the slur was being used to describe Emma. And then, just a second later, he realized that such a thing could never be true, and the pain he felt was almost as strong as to convince him that he was losing her a second time. He fought through the surging sorrow, trying to streamline his thoughts in order to focus on what the message *really* communicated.

Victor was no linguist, but to him, it sounded like yet another kidnapping had taken place right under his nose. He supposed that was obvious, but it was also completely unbelievable. He had a million questions: Why Maddie? What was the kidnapper's intention? Had Crane been lying to cover up for the person who had really murdered Emma? Why did the kidnapper want to meet back at the church?

Victor couldn't answer any of those questions if he just kept standing here and was wasting time. Maddie could be in a dire situation, and he might have the chance to save her.

He had been too late for Emma.

He wouldn't be too late for Maddie, too.

Victor dropped the photograph and ran out of the apartment. He realized that he should probably call 911 and tell them about what had happened, how he was being summoned to the church while Maddie was missing, and how they needed to get to the church and look for her before it was too late. And yet…

I want to face this fucker alone.

Whoever would be waiting for him at the church must have had a hand in Emma's death, and if that was the case, Victor was going to give him the same fate as the fate Crane had met. He wasn't afraid because he had nothing left to lose. Maddie was a friend, and he wanted to save her, but this was mostly about revenge. He was going back to Our Lady of Perpetual Grace to finish this. *This ends today.* And, just like he had done with his efforts to find Emma, he would do it without the help of the police.

As much as it pained him not to leave immediately, he knew he needed to clean up and change his dirty clothing to avoid any questioning as he traveled back to the church on foot. Under the warm water of the shower, the grime and blood washed off of his body as he scrubbed himself furiously, the cut on his hand once again opening and beginning to bleed. As he got out of the shower, he dug through the bathroom drawers, finding Band-Aids that wouldn't truly be enough for the injury but might at least keep the wound tight enough that it might stop bleeding again. Giving up on the bandages, he plodded into the kitchen, lit up the stovetop, and took one of the kitchen knives to the flame. After it heated up, he pressed it hard into the cut on his palm, the oozes of plasma sizzling before the skin cauterized, sealing the slice. He washed his hands haphazardly, and after putting on clean jeans and a clean shirt, he headed out of the door with haste.

Chapter Seventeen

Victor spent some time staking out the church from across the street, concealing himself behind a line of parked cars to ensure that he wouldn't draw any attention to himself. There wasn't a single cop in sight around the church, which puzzled him a great deal. No doubt, the police were looking for the man who killed Crane, learning about the bodies. Victor didn't even want to think about that; it was probably best that he didn't. He had to concentrate on finding Maddie now, and then, once that was done and whoever was bent on holding his life hostage was taken care of, he could face the police. Sleepy morning traffic, dedicated joggers, and passersby occasionally showed, but the more he looked, the more obvious it seemed that there hadn't been any police activity. He hadn't seen anyone come or go from the interior or even the parking lot. Could it really be so simple to just waltz right up the door and go in?

If I wait any longer, whoever wanted me to come here might leave, Victor thought, gritting his teeth. *And if I miss them, who knows what will happen to Maddie?*

That was certainly a concern because he wasn't sure how long it had been since Maddie had been snatched from her own apartment, and he doubted very much that Maddie's captor was the sort of person who would forgive being stood up. No, the more he thought about it, the more reasons he saw to stop waiting for there to be a problem and to just take his opportunity while he still had the luxury of making a choice.

Victor waited until the traffic was clear enough for him to cross the street before doing so at a run, making a beeline to the front doors of the church. He almost expected someone to tackle him from behind or jump in front of him to stop him from reaching his goal, but no one did. He reached the front of the church, wrenched the door open, and flung himself inside without having crossed the path of a single person. Regardless, he immediately ducked down when he got inside, listening for footsteps or signs that someone had seen him.

The seconds ticked past, but the only thing that Victor could hear was his own heartbeat in his ears. Somehow, miraculously, he had made it to the church without raising a single eyebrow, which felt wrong, considering that this place should have been an active crime scene after the mess he made of Edward Crane. Why was he here, on his own, in an empty building that should be swarming with police officers?

It doesn't matter, Victor told himself, standing up and turning away from the church doors to face the pews and altar down the aisle. *They could have been abducted by aliens, for all I care. I'm here to finish something that never should have been started, not stand around trying to piece together whatever the hell the cops do with their free time.*

Victor took a step deeper into the church, his senses on high alert. The young daylight was streaming in through the stained glass windows, but it was still shadowy and difficult to see. Victor took a few more cautious steps forward, scanning the room for movement and finding one. He stopped where he was, trying to decide what this meant. On the surface, the church was completely empty, and it very well could be; Victor had taken so long to get here that the asshole he was after might have left just like he had feared. But no— what was that down there beside the altar?

Victor jogged to the altar and saw that someone had left a flickering candle there. A rich red one, large and likely only used for special occasions and the holidays. It hadn't been burning for long; there wasn't too much wax dribbling down the side, and the liquid wax pooling in the center was still shallow. A candle by itself didn't mean much, but it gave Victor a prickling feeling along his spine. He knew where the church stored candles like this, which meant…

Slowly, carefully, Victor turned to look at the door that led to the back room where he had found Father Hudson's address book earlier. The door stood open, though the inside of the room beyond was shrouded in blackness. Victor was debating whether it was more brave or stupid to enter when Father Hudson emerged from the blackness, catching Victor entirely off guard. He must have just been standing in there, watching Victor silently while Victor stared unseeingly back at him.

"Father!" he exclaimed, taking a few steps backward. "What are you doing here? Excuse my language, but you damn near scared the shit out of me."

"I think we both know what I'm doing here, Victor."

It took all of a second for Victor to make the connection, and when he did, it hit him like a brick in the gut. He almost winced from the impact, but he knew better than to show any sign of weakness while facing off with Maddie's kidnapper.

"Where is she?" Victor demanded through gritted teeth.

Father Hudson just smiled wanly, a dark twinkle to his eye.

"I swear, Hudson, if she's… if she's dead, I'll send you to burn with Edward Crane."

"I think you'll find that it's difficult to scare me with promises of fire and brimstone, Victor, so skip it. I want to cut to the good stuff and stop wasting time. You never thought I had a part in this, did you? Be honest. You never knew that it could be me."

Victor said nothing, but that was as good as admitting that he hadn't, apparently, because Hudson's smile widened.

"You stupid fucking redneck. When you left last night, I'd thought you'd called the police, but you didn't! And you weren't even smart enough to call them now. I'm going to plant it all on you," Hudson laughed. "Crane's death. All the *whores* buried beneath the coffins. Jesus Christ, you're stupid! From the day we first met, I could tell that you're an ignorant, simple-minded man. I told you then that revenge would blind you, and now you're standing her to meet your maker. You're definitely nowhere near being as smart as your degenerate daughter was. From what I understand, she was exceptional until the very end, even if it was at stripping. Her death must be a blow to you, but it might ease your pain to think of her death in a different light. After all, God does not weep over the death of whores. Edward and I were simply purifying the city in which we live, and the Lord smiles upon us for it!"

Victor was almost speechless with revulsion.

Almost.

"You're sick, Hudson," he spat. "You're a fucked up old man who couldn't be farther away from God. I don't give a shit either way, though, to be honest. I'm still going to make you pay for what you did and what Edward did."

"Careful, Victor," Hudson said, raising a finger. "You think you're in control here, but you're not. I'm the one calling the shots. Don't dupe yourself into believing that you have the upper hand. Besides, don't you have questions? Don't you want to know why we did it and how? How we picked her, Victor?"

Victor wanted to snap at this lunatic priest that no, he didn't want to know any of the horrific details of his daughter's murder, but something dark in him *did* want to know. He wanted every excuse to rip the man in front of him to shreds, and he also wanted to have this one last tie to Emma, to have some sort of an idea of what she went through while he had been back at home, drinking the day away. To torture himself in this way might be the only way he could repent for what he hadn't done for her. It didn't matter that he had managed to track her down after her death, that he had gotten this far with only the help of her former roommate. He had still been too late, and maybe he wouldn't have been if he hadn't been too distant to even have a phone she could reach him on.

"Victor? Are you still with us?" Hudson inquired, breaking Victor's despondent train of thought. "Please pay attention. It's not as much fun if you aren't listening."

"Fine," Victor said venomously. "Enlighten me."

It's weird that he wants to share any of this with me at all, Victor thought, frowning to himself. He recognized that the thought had some sort of importance, but for now, all of his attention was directed towards Hudson.

"She wasn't our first, but you're the first one who was able to track her down like you did. Maybe we got lazy. Most of these whores don't have families who care about them, not more than a couple of kids or something that they've resorted to a life of sin to feed. We aren't used to people trying to find the sluts we kidnap, and we definitely aren't used to people with your level of dedication coming after us. If I had known that—what was her name? Emma?—had a father like you, I might have asked Edward to choose a different target. But, as things were, we went ahead with our selection, and look where that got us. My half-brother is lying dead in my own cemetery with his head bashed in, and I'm face to face with the criminal who did it. This fine day could hardly be more exciting."

For a moment, Victor couldn't quite follow what Hudson meant when he referred to his half-brother, but then he realized that the man he referred to could be no other than Crane. That explained the picture that had been at his apartment, the one with the message scrawled across the back that had led him back here. The boys in the photograph must have been Crane and Hudson as children, which made the woman standing behind them Hudson's mother. For all Victor knew, that picture was of Hudson and Crane saying some last goodbyes before Hudson's new parents took him to his new home. The tale about Crane going through the foster care system was probably true as well, as was the bit about him acting as a groundskeeper for the church. After all, Victor had seen his handiwork first-hand.

"So, what, then? You called me here for revenge? Is that what this is?" Victor asked at last.

"No, not quite," Hudson replied thoughtfully. "It's more as a means of self-preservation."

"How do you figure?"

"Well, depending on what they learn, the police may decide to dig and find some very incriminating evidence of exactly what it looks like we've been doing in our cemetery. But it's not over for me because I'll have captured the murderer of Edward Crane and Maddie Rose. If they never learn of the other bodies, I'm in the clear. Even if they do somehow suspect something else is happening here, there's a good chance that if I blame this entirely on you and Crane, I can get away with it. I'll look like a silly old fool who can't see a serial killer underneath his own nose, but I'll take the damage to my reputation over having my freedom revoked any day of the week."

"Okay, that's great, but what the hell do you need me for? All I want is my daughter's body back so I can take her home, and that's what I'm getting. I don't need to know every single detail of what you've been up to this whole time."

And as he said it, that important little thought revisited Victor again: *It's weird that he wants to share this with me. Why? Why is he doing this?*

"You haven't put two and two together yet? I suppose I shouldn't be surprised. Like I said, I'm aware that you aren't the brightest candle on the altar."

As he said this, Victor *did* put two and two together, and he could feel his fight or flight instinct engage.

"I'm a loose end," he said. "We could talk and undo everything that you want to establish in a heartbeat."

"*There* we go. I'm proud of you, Victor. I didn't even have to spell it out for you. I was getting worried." He smiled, then cracked his knuckles. "Is there anything in particular that you would like to say, Victor? Now would be the perfect time."

"Yeah, there is one thing: leave Maddie out of this. Let her go. I'm the one you want."

"Not before we have some fun!" Hudson exclaimed.

With absolutely no warning, Hudson began to pummel him. Unlike the adversaries Victor had fought recently, Hudson knew how to handle himself. His blows were deliberate and precise, striking Victor first in the solar plexus, knocking the wind out of him, and causing him to double over. Then, while Victor had his head down, Hudson kneed Victor in the face, causing blood to spurt from his nose in rivers. The pain on its own was enough to stop Victor from thinking properly, but he was still reeling from the initial attack. As he got his wits about him, the vicious man of God backed off, laughing.

"It's not as fun if you don't even try!" he goaded. "Come on, Victor. Get one shot in. Hit me!"

Victor thought about the fate of his daughter, the kidnapping of her roommate, and the fact that if he didn't win this fight, he was going to die. Gritting his teeth against all of the pain he was already in, he threw a punch at waiting Hudson. Apparently, however, Hudson hadn't been inviting him to take a *free* punch: he grabbed Victor's arm while it was still in the air and redirected his momentum so that he slammed against the wall, rattling the furniture. Hudson then grabbed Victor's shoulders and threw him to the floor, throwing a kick at Victor's ribs for good measure.

Victor could hardly think. He knew that he was getting the shit beaten out of him, but that was about the only thing he could concentrate on right now. He tried to curl himself into a ball to protect himself, but Hudson wrenched him apart and stood with a foot on his chest, slowly squeezing the air out of him. Victor began to feel light-headed, and even though he was making efforts to get the priest the hell off of him, black spots began to appear in his vision. The spots grew larger and larger, ballooning up so much that they blocked everything from view. And then, Victor didn't feel anything at all.

. . .

Victor was behind the wheel of his truck, driving down the country road that led into town from the farmhouse. Raindrops hammered the windshield so intensely that the wipers couldn't keep up with them. The fruiting wheat thrashed unrelentingly, the flowering heads of wheat whipping about, tearing off into the wind like a million little arrowheads flying through the sky in a frantic battlefield full of invisible soldiers. The truck rocked as it was buffeted by wind so strong that Victor felt as though he were driving through a hurricane. He looked for the headlights that he knew would be waiting for him down the road, gradually growing closer until that inevitable collision, but they seemed to be swallowed up by the storm: Victor couldn't find them.

"Victor."

Victor turned his head towards the passenger's seat, and what he saw surprised him so much that he almost crashed the truck himself. It was Lily sitting there, just like she always was, but this time it was *really* Lily: the features on her face were distinct, and the look in her jade eyes—that expression of warmth, of love, and the intangible magic that lingered behind the eyes of the living. It was all there. *She* was all there. Victor felt his own eyes welling up with tears of joy, but Lily put her hand on his shoulder before he could open his mouth and tell her one of the millions of things he had wanted to say to her since she had died.

"We don't have much time, so you're going to have to just listen," Lily went on.

"I don't know if I can do that. I've missed you so much, Lily."

"Please, Victor."

"But Lily," Victor said, gesturing to the road in front of them. "There's no truck coming for us this time. Look for yourself! Nothing's there."

"Maybe not anymore," Lily conceded, "but it's not your time yet. Victor... I am so *proud* of you for how far you've gone to save our little family, to protect what little of it is left. You are twice the man I married, and you swept me off my feet even then. But you have to go just a little farther. You can't let that monster of a man do to Maddie what he did to Emma and all of the other women lying in that cemetery. You have to go and save her and bring closure to their souls."

"I want to stay here with you," Victor choked out.

"It's okay," Lily said with a small smile. "I'm not going anywhere."

She leaned to the side and planted her lips on Victor's cheek, and when she did, Victor closed his eyes, savoring the feeling of such a simple expression of love that he had forgotten, which made him feel so light. In fact, everything was growing lighter—the clouds were breaking up, and the rain had slowed to a drizzle, bringing his attention back to the road and making him notice that the headlights he hadn't seen before were perhaps ten feet away from him. He opened his mouth to scream, but the car hit just before he could make a sound, and then—

• • •

PAIN. Lots of it.

Victor slowly blinked his eyes open and drew a shaky breath, trying to get his bearings. His body felt as though it had been hit by a train, and that reminded him that Father Hudson might be around where he was somewhere, so he had better be quiet about being awake unless he wanted another beating. Slowly, he allowed his eyes to explore the room, and he realized just as quickly that he was exactly where he had passed out. He also realized that he was alone, at least for the moment.

Warily, Victor tried to get to his feet, but he was immediately punished by a fresh wave of agony radiating from his right leg. He clamped a hand over his mouth to stop him from screaming and stared wide-eyed at his leg as though that might help him discover the reason for his pain. Cautiously, he bit his hand and tried putting a little pressure on it again.

Ow, fuck, fuck, fuck!

It didn't take a genius to figure out that the leg was probably broken, maybe from falling funny, maybe from something that Hudson had done after Victor had passed out. The reason wasn't really important. What *was* important was the fact that this was going to seriously inhibit him from being able to get out of the church alive, which was really bad considering that the odds hadn't looked great to begin with. Victor might have spent more time mulling this over if a wail from just behind him hadn't immediately caught his attention.

"Please, *stop!*"

It was Maddie's voice. Victor turned around slowly—both because he now knew that Hudson was in the room and for the sake of his leg—and saw Hudson standing in front of him, back turned. He was facing Maddie, who was sitting in a chair, likely bound there judging by the way her arms looked. Most of Victor's view was obscured by Hudson, but when he moved slightly to the side, Maddie's face became visible. It was twisted in pain, her cheeks streaked with mascara tears. Victor couldn't tell what Hudson was doing to her, but seeing her in so much distress was terrible. When she screamed, Victor heard Emma's voice, and his chest seized up. When he saw a splatter of blood stain the floor, Victor could no longer restrain himself. Even if it meant losing his own life, he had to do something to save Maddie from whatever horror she was experiencing.

"Hey, asshole! Leave her alone!"

Father Hudson turned around, a cruel smile plastered on his blood-spattered face.

"Feeling better, are we?" Hudson asked, walking towards Victor. When he reached him, he gave Victor a friendly nod before stepping on his broken leg. Victor howled with agony, and Hudson yelled over him:

"What are you going to do about it? Nothing!"

Hudson turned back to Maddie, whose eyes were about the size of plates and fixed on Victor's.

"H… help me!" she stammered out of a bloody mouth.

Victor didn't hesitate. He began to drag himself across the floor towards her, which Hudson seemed to think was very amusing. He took a moment away from whatever he was preparing to continue doing to Maddie—pulling teeth, it looked like—and looked down at Victor, laughing.

"You look like a maggot!" he crowed.

"Please, spare her!" Victor begged. "I don't care what you do with me, but let her go. She hasn't done anything. She didn't do anything to Crane—nothing. It was all me!"

Hudson snorted, delivering Victor yet another kick in the ribs. Victor curled up automatically against the pain and waited for more, but Hudson had already returned his attention to Maddie, not dignifying Victor's pleas with an answer. She squirmed in her seat, thrashing to get free, and her panic made Victor feel panicked, too. He knew that Hudson was just going to keep torturing her needlessly unless he did something, but he felt so useless. How was he supposed to do anything when he was trapped on the floor like this?

The Derringer!

Victor had utterly forgotten that he had a little gun tucked away, invisible in his baggy jeans. At this close of range, he could easily kill Hudson with it if he got the right shot… though the odds of that happening weren't looking great. The best he could do without standing up would be to shoot out the back of one of his legs, so that's what he did. As the Derringer fired, a loud cracking noise making a deafening sound, Hudson collapsed to the floor at once, screaming in agony, and Victor seized his opportunity. He beat the fallen priest with the gun, using as much force as he could muster, pouring his anger into every strike. Hudson wasn't able to defend himself from Victor's blows, but even with his wrecked leg, he was already beginning to regain composure; he was trying to wrestle the gun out of Victor's hands. The gun went flying across the room as Victor and Hudson wrestled for control of the situation. Victor knew he had to kill the priest or… he couldn't bear to think what would happen to Maddie after Hudson had finished having his fun with her.

No, that couldn't happen.

So, Victor followed his instincts and reached for the priest's neck. He fought through his own agony to follow a makeshift plan, knowing that if he eased up at all, Hudson would gain the upper hand in no time. Hudson was almost unscathed, and Victor was all but beaten to a pulp. But, thanks to his weight and perhaps the grace of God Himself, Victor was able to get on top of Hudson, who was snarling and tearing at him like a feral animal. Victor fearlessly went in for the rosary hanging from the priest's neck, shoving it against the flesh of Hudson's throat. Hudson gasped and choked, and even though Victor might have drawn pleasure from this—after all, Hudson had essentially done the same thing to him—he looked away in disgust. Victor was a fighter, he was a drunk, and he would have made a damn good detective, but he wasn't a murderer. There was no sweetness to this moment, but it was one that had to come for Maddie's sake, if not for his own.

Hudson struggled more frantically, trying to pry the rosary away from his neck, but Victor just pressed harder. Shortly thereafter, Hudson began to weaken, and then, a few moments later, he laid still. Victor continued to choke him, aware that it could be a facade or that there was a chance that Hudson wasn't completely dead. Finally, the rosary broke, and beads scattered across the floor of the church.

He waited as if in a trance, standing between the mortal and divine planes, the sounds of Maddie thrashing and screaming in the background drowned out by a ringing in his ears that left him unable to act. Time slipped by like grains of sand in an hourglass, and then, at last, Victor noticed that he was awfully out of breath and his vision was beginning to double and slip away from him. He knew he was going to pass out an instant before he did, but that didn't stop the blackness from swallowing him up again. He could only hope that he would see Lily here again.

CHAPTER EIGHTEEN

"Victor!" a soft voice broke the silence. "Victor?"

Victor thought he heard the sound of Lily's voice waking him up from a nap on the couch after a long day tending the fields, but as his eyes groggily opened, bright fluorescent lights made it hard for him to gain focus. A wretched soreness fell upon him as his senses started flooding back in, and the smell of antiseptic and day's old perfume flooded his nostrils.

"Victor! You're awake," the voice came again. As his eyes finally regained their faculty, he saw Maddie's weary-looking face standing above him. Despite her youth and beauty, she looked disheveled and worn down, as if she hadn't slept in days. She fell upon him in an attempt to hug him, sending spasms of pain throughout his sore body. Despite this, he feebly wrapped an arm around her as she cried softly into his chest.

"What happened? Are you okay?" Victor croaked as the beeping machine next to him indicated that he was apparently alive and in a hospital.

When Maddie lifted herself away from him and slumped into the chair she'd undoubtedly stayed in by his side, Victor took in the full view of the hospital room's white walls and floors and realized there was no window. At the door stood a police officer standing guard, no doubt because Victor had killed two men and would have to face the judicial system.

"Victor," Maddie started, stumbling over her words as she babbled. "You saved my life. After the priest… after you passed out… I was able to get to the tools and found a way to cut away the ropes, and…" Maddie started crying uncontrollably.

"And you called 911 and got me help," Victor finished the thought for her with a soft, fatherly tone in his voice. "Thank you, Maddie. I'm so glad you're…"

"The police know everything!" she blurted out. "I told them everything the priest said… about Emma… they know why you did it! I had to tell them."

Victor held out a hand for Maddie to stop and repeated, "Thank you, Maddie."

His wounds had been treated, his broken leg now in a cast, his ribs throbbing in pain, and his head still spinning. Now that the nasty business was over, he felt the weight of everything crashing down on him physically, mentally, and spiritually. Still, he put on a brave face as he spoke to Maddie about how brave she had been and how great of a person she was, both as a friend to Emma and to himself. He heard the officer from the door speaking to someone, but he didn't bother to listen. Surely, now that he was awake, there would be a detective in soon to speak to him about his side of the story, and he would need to face the consequences of his actions. No sooner had he taken account of his new life post-Emma than two detectives walked into the door, a man and woman dressed well in business attire, brandishing their badges already in their hands.

"Victor Nash," one of them said, "I'm Detective Erik Jacksen, and this is Detective Ian Olsen."

"It's good to see you again, Maddie. How are you holding up?" Detective Olsen addressed her. Without waiting for an answer, she motioned towards the door, "We'd like to speak to Mr. Nash alone if you don't mind."

"Can't really say I'm good," Maddie muttered as she pushed herself up from the chair slowly, clearly uncomfortable around the police. "Victor, I've already told them everything," she added, nodding at him before scuttling out of the door and past the officer on guard duty.

"Let me start by saying that I'm sorry for your loss," Officer Jacksen said as Officer Olsen closed the door behind Maddie.

Victor wanted to shout at them and tell them how the police hadn't taken the disappearance of his daughter seriously, that he was forced to react, that they'd allowed a serial killer to run amuck in Minneapolis for God knows how fucking long. But he felt defeated and saw no real purpose in fighting anyone anymore. It wouldn't get him Emma back, and it would only serve to make it harder for him to bury her body properly and pay the respects she deserved.

After Victor relayed his story and answered their barrage of questions, he finally asked the only thing he wanted to know, "Did you find Emma?"

CHAPTER NINETEEN

Following Victor's stay in the hospital, he went through a blur of rushed court dates, leading to him making bail and a pending trial for charges of vigilantism that would take place in a few months' time. Given the circumstances, and Victor deemed not to be a risk to the public, he was granted permission to take Emma back to Hope River, and Maddie insisted that Victor stay with her until Emma's body was cleared and prepared for the journey home.

The first thing he had done when he got released from the hospital and was no longer sitting in a cell was go out for a bottle of whiskey to wash some of the pills down with, and when he arrived back at the apartment and walked into Emma's room, he lost it a little. In all his pain, all he could do was take a handful of his pills and drop to his knees, screaming in hopes that his cries to God would bring him some semblance of peace. But, alas, all it brought with it was more pain and suffering. Maddie had helped him into the bed, and he had finished off his whiskey, drifting off to a fantasy that was heaven compared to the hell he was living.

Maddie didn't bring up Victor's meltdown, and Victor didn't bring up any of the times he had heard her sobbing in her room between her shifts, sometimes screaming into pillows. They pretended that everything was normal, that their loss of Emma was the greatest trauma either of them had suffered recently, and that they were in the midst of flowing through the natural stages of grief. Victor knew that they didn't fool anyone, but faking it helped some.

With Emma's body finally ready for transport, the night before Victor was set to catch the train back home, Victor and Maddie were sitting down on the couch in the living room of Maddie's apartment, watching a TV show that neither of them seemed too interested in when Maddie broke the semi-quiet.

"I think I'm going to quit dancing," she said without looking away from the television screen.

Victor was surprised, but he kept the conversation blasé. "*Hm.* Any reason why or just because?"

"Nah, I don't know. I've just been doing some thinking, that's all. I think I might try to go to college."

"What for?" Victor asked warmly.

"Criminal justice," Maddie said, choking back the tears welling up in her eyes.

She didn't elaborate further, and Victor didn't ask her to. He thought he already knew the answer, and he wasn't going to make her go into detail about how her encounter with Father Hudson had made her rethink her life choices.

The two of them didn't say another word to each other until they simultaneously decided that it was time for bed. Victor had just hauled himself up off the couch when Maddie paused at the mouth of the hallway leading to the bedrooms beyond.

"Hey, Victor?"

"Yeah?"

"I wish that my dad had loved me half as much as you love

Emma. I know that things got weird between you two over the last couple of months or whatever, but… I can tell that you really care about her. I miss her, but I can't imagine what you've been feeling."

"Thanks, Maddie. I appreciate that."

"No, Victor, I'm serious. I don't just let strange men hang around my apartment for days and days on end if I don't think they're quality people."

"Well, I don't know about my quality, Maddie, but you're right about how much I love Emma. Without her…"

He trailed off, unable to finish his thought, and Maddie didn't make him.

"I want you to stop drinking," she said suddenly. "For Emma. I think she would have really liked that."

Victor had smiled emptily. "You know, I bet she would have," he said. "I might have to give that a shot."

But he knew that he wouldn't.

Saying goodbye to Maddie the next morning felt very bittersweet. Leaving without bringing her back to Hope River almost seemed wrong. He'd asked if she wanted to come to attend Emma's funeral, but Maddie decided she couldn't bear another heartbreak so soon. Victor didn't push the issue. As they gave each other a warm hug, she said, "You better come and stay with me when you're back for your trial."

The train ride went faster than Victor had expected, and before he knew it, he was back in familiar territory. He felt a rush of relief as he stared out the window, watching the world stop flitting by as the train slowed to a halt. He saw Harry standing on the platform, waiting for him, with Dakota standing beside him on a leash. Ordinarily, Victor would have felt happy to see the two of them, but the emotion just didn't come this time. The muscles that would have pulled his mouth into a smile remained slack.

Harry bear-hugged Victor as soon as he stepped off the train, giving him the biggest hug that Victor had probably received in his life. Pain shot throughout his battered body, and he nearly dropped his crutches, but the two of them let Dakota whine and jump up on his hind legs, scratching at the two of them with his front paws as though he wanted in on the embrace. There was only so long that the brothers could comfortably touch each other, so they drew apart, and an inevitable awkward silence descended over them. Neither of them really wanted to talk about what had happened to the dead girl who was carefully being unloaded from the train as they stood there, and yet it was impossible never to address the subject. In the end, Harry just told Victor that he had brought Victor's truck to the station so they wouldn't have to worry about fitting Emma's "container" inside a car, and that was about as much as they cared to talk about it. Emma ended up in the back of Victor's truck with Dakota there to watch over her, and Victor and Harry had ridden in silence all the way to the farmhouse.

Harry made most of the arrangements for the funeral. Victor was physically and mentally exhausted, and, knowing this, Harry stepped up and saved his big brother. It was a closed-casket service for obvious reasons, and the event took place on some open land at the farm. Victor dug his daughter's grave himself, so he was sure it was safe and comfortable down there, a nice place for Emma to rediscover her connection to the Earth. When he and Harry buried her, he expected to feel soul-rattling pain, but he felt something else entirely.

She's calling to me, he realized. *Both of them are.*

When everything was said and done, and Emma was where she needed to be, Victor told Harry that he needed to go inside and rest a while.

"Take as long as you need," Harry said. "Should I stay around, or do you want me to head home? I'm not sure you should be alone during a time like this."

"I'm doing okay, Harry. Dakota can keep me company from here on out."

"You sure?"

"I'm sure. Thanks for taking care of him, by the way. I appreciate that."

"It's no problem!" Harry said, rubbing Dakota behind the ears. "He's a good boy, isn't he? What a good boy!"

Victor just smiled.

Soon, Harry was driving down the dirt road back to the main street, and Victor and Dakota were alone once more at the farmhouse. Victor hobbled to his front porch and took a few minutes to look around the sections of the farm before him. There were still crops here, but it was nothing like the thriving agricultural paradise he had maintained for so many years. He closed his eyes and tried to recapture the feeling of farming, that joy of having a purpose that had been extinguished in him for so long, but he came away unsuccessful. He wasn't disappointed, exactly; this was more or less what he had expected. Instead, he was acceptant, and he turned around and walked inside his house on his crutches.

It was good to be back, especially now that the place was spick and span. In addition to taking care of Dakota, Harry had cleaned up the place for Victor, maybe as a welcome home gift, maybe as a way of paying his respects to Emma, who wouldn't have wanted to live in filth. Whatever the reason, it was nice to stand in the sunny living room like this. He could almost hear Lily asking him to slip his shoes off at the door, but as things were, he wore his boots inside and limped slowly in and out of each of the rooms, taking in his home. It didn't feel that way anymore—like a home. It was more of a house now that he was the only person in his little family left.

Victor picked up a picture of his family from his bedroom wall and carried it with him back to the living room. He gingerly sat down on the couch, grateful for the bottle of whiskey he had left on the coffee table. It looked like there was enough left to do the job. Dakota, who had been following him all through the farmhouse, jumped up on the couch beside him and put his head in his lap. Victor smiled and gave the dog a solid pat.

"Good boy, Dakota."

Dakota's tail thumped.

Victor sat there for a while, nursing his bottle of whiskey. His leg and ribs started to ache, so he took out his pills and shook a few onto his hand. He stared at them for a minute before downing them and shaking more onto his palm, again and again until the bottle was empty. He sucked down as much whiskey as he could hold before he sank into a familiar, foggy stupor… but maybe this *wasn't* so familiar. It was deeper. Deeper than he had ever brought himself before. It was like being thrown into the deep end of a pool with his hands tied, and though a part of him demanded that he struggle, the dominant part of him allowed himself to slip under the water and drift down, down, down…

• • •

WHEN VICTOR OPENED HIS EYES AGAIN, he was behind the wheel of his truck. This time, however, there was no storm. The sun beamed down on the country road before him like the smile of God Himself, and lush, tall crops of golden wheat waved in the gentle breeze on both sides as the truck bumped along. Victor realized in an intrinsic sort of way that he didn't have to hold onto the steering wheel or pay attention to where he was headed, so he took a few long moments to stare out his window at the seemingly endless fields of spring wheat that he somehow knew was his. It was a better year than he had ever seen, and he was still wondering how he had done it when he felt a hand slide into his lap. He looked over to the passenger's seat, and saw, of course, Lily sitting there, smiling at him. Warmth flooded back into the hole where Victor's heart had once been, and he clasped her hand, smiling back at her with tears in his eyes.

"Lily," he said, "how did we do this? How are we possibly going to be able to bring in all of this harvest?"

"You don't have to worry about that anymore," Lily said, squeezing his hand softly.

"What do you mean?"

"Look."

She pointed ahead through the windshield, and when she did, Victor fully expected to be stricken by the other vehicle that always destroyed the brief, imaginary conversations he had with his wife. He even tensed up, but nothing came. Puzzled, but relieved, he looked where Lily was indicating and saw that there *was* no car. He could see clear down the road for miles, and there wasn't anybody coming towards him. Not for a very long time, at least.

"Where'd he go?" Victor asked, turning back to Lily.

"Far away, and he's not coming back."

This news took some time to sink in for Victor, but when it did, he pulled his wife into his arms and buried his face in her sweet-smelling hair, believing—dare he say "knowing" now?—that he wouldn't have to leave her this time. When he released her at last, she had tears in her eyes, too, and he wiped one pooling on her bottom lashes with his thumb.

"Are you ready, Victor?" Lily inquired, taking his hand in hers.

"Ready for what?"

"Ready to go home."

But the voice that replied wasn't Lily's. Victor twisted around to look into the backseat and saw Emma sitting there. Emma, as Victor had known her before he had lost her to drugs and stripping. His All-American Emma. She smiled at him, and Victor felt complete. Whole. Whole in a way that he had been certain he would never feel again.

"Yes, honey," he said at last. "It's time to go home."

www.ingramcontent.com/pod-product-compliance
Lightning Source LLC
Chambersburg PA
CBHW071115100726
47908CB00008B/2382